108課綱、全民英檢中高級適用

英語 Make Me High 系列

30天計畫PLUS⁺：
打造 進階 英文字彙題本

丁雍嫺 邢雯桂 盧思嘉 應惠蕙 編著

附解析本

丁雍嫻
學歷／國立臺灣師範大學英語學系學士
　　　國立臺灣師範大學英語學系研究所暑期班
經歷／國立新竹女子高級中學

邢雯桂
學歷／國立中央大學英美語文學系學士
　　　美國新罕布夏大學英語教學碩士
經歷／國立新竹女子高級中學

盧思嘉
學歷／國立彰化師範大學英語學系學士
　　　英國伯明罕大學英語教學碩士
經歷／國立新竹女子高級中學

應惠蕙
學歷／國立臺灣師範大學英語學系學士
　　　國立臺灣師範大學英語學系碩士
經歷／國立新竹女子高級中學
　　　華東臺商子女學校

三民書局

序

英語 Make Me High 系列的理想在於超越，在於創新。

這是時代的精神，也是我們出版的動力；

這是教育的目的，也是我們進步的執著。

針對英語的全球化與未來的升學趨勢，

我們設計了一系列適合普高、技高學生的英語學習書籍。

面對英語，不會徬徨不再迷惘，學習的心徹底沸騰，

心情好 High！

實戰模擬，掌握先機知己知彼，百戰不殆決勝未來，

分數更 High！

選擇優質的英語學習書籍，才能激發學習的強烈動機；

興趣盎然便不會畏懼艱難，自信心要自己大聲說出來。

本書如良師指引循循善誘，如益友相互鼓勵攜手成長。

展書輕閱，你將發現……

學習英語原來也可以這麼 High！

前　言

　　《30 天計畫 PLUS：打造進階英文字彙題本》由作者群針對大考中心頒布之高中英文參考詞彙表 5–6 級進階字彙為主軸，精心編寫而成。全書共分 30 回，每回 25 題，其中含 20 回進階字彙試題，8 回字彙總複習，2 回實力延伸 PLUS 字彙試題，題型包括以下三大類型：

Ⅰ. Multiple Choice（字彙題，15 題）

　　測驗學生對英文單句的理解程度及各單字的熟悉度。

Ⅱ. Fill in the Blank（字彙填空，5 題）

　　評量學生對詞組及慣用語的運用程度。

Ⅲ. Guided Translation（引導式翻譯，5 題）

　　檢視學生是否熟稔單字、片語，進而將其運用於句子內。

　　透過這些題型，將可由點、線、面全方位檢核學生的字彙實力。

　　本手冊的使用方式不拘。學生可先研讀三民出版的單字書《進階英文字彙力 4501~6000》、《學測英文字彙力 6000 PLUS 隨身讀》，於熟悉各單字之用法後，再以本書驗收學習成果；亦可直接利用本書，於學測前 30 天寫題衝刺，檢視較不熟悉的字詞。無論何種方式，相信皆能增強讀者們的字彙能力。

　　字彙乃語文之本，能通曉各單字的意義、掌握重要單字的用法，則各式題型的測驗皆不足為懼。期望本書能對正在準備考試的莘莘學子們有所助益。

Table of Contents

練習完一個回次後，你可以在該回次的◯打勾並在 <u>12/31</u> 填寫完成日期。

• 圖片來源：Shutterstock

Round 1

I. Multiple Choice

(   ) 1. If you plan to be a lawyer, you'll have to learn to stop _____ and speak loudly and clearly.

     (A) mumbling   (B) rattling   (C) moaning   (D) peeking

(   ) 2. Fiona is always late and never works hard. I am _____ about her chances of promotion.

     (A) superstitious   (B) passionate   (C) indignant   (D) skeptical

(   ) 3. Boxton got promoted because his boss saw him as a great _____ to the company.

     (A) lieutenant   (B) asset   (C) janitor   (D) estate

(   ) 4. Autumn leaves _____ in the wind. It looks like they are about to fall any minute.

     (A) dazzle   (B) paddle   (C) smash   (D) quiver

(   ) 5. The _____ of Bill's affair with his secretary ruined his political career.

     (A) disclosure   (B) revenue   (C) assessment   (D) prohibition

(   ) 6. Jade is very _____ about critical social theories. You can always seek her counsel when you have difficulties with your assignment.

     (A) honorable   (B) advisory

     (C) lofty   (D) knowledgeable

(   ) 7. Jessie felt a _____ in her throat when she bid farewell to her son at the airport.

     (A) lump   (B) sponge   (C) novice   (D) mammal

(　　) 8. It came as no surprise to learn that the heavy smoker had been _____ with lung cancer.

    (A) distracted   (B) dictated   (C) diagnosed   (D) disabled

(　　) 9. Susie used a _____ to transfer some photos onto her computer.

    (A) cashier   (B) scanner   (C) seminar   (D) coupon

(　　) 10. The old man often _____ on the good old days. He thinks all too much about them.

    (A) perceives   (B) disgraces   (C) dwells   (D) modifies

(　　) 11. The loss of the priceless jewels greatly _____ the shopkeeper.

    (A) dismayed   (B) disciplined   (C) disconnected   (D) discharged

(　　) 12. In the past, middle-class women used to wear _____ that often made them feel very restrained.

    (A) garments   (B) sandals   (C) suitcases   (D) perfumes

(　　) 13. The value of the tall building has never _____ owing to its perfect location in the city center.

    (A) manifested   (B) diminished   (C) abounded   (D) complied

(　　) 14. Nowadays, more and more people are engaging in workouts in the hope of _____ a few kilos.

    (A) shedding   (B) flipping   (C) patching   (D) slaying

(　　) 15. The industrial detergent can clean dirty and greasy _____ and make them look brand new.

    (A) tiles   (B) corals   (C) episodes   (D) fuses

II. Fill In the Blank （從下方選出適合字彙做適當變化，填入答案）

abundant	apt	midst	mainstream	turmoil

_____ 1. People's lives are under pressure in the _____ of epidemics, climate change, and wars.

_____ 2. The island is _____ in rare species of tropical plants, which is one of its attractions.

_____ 3. Train transportation was in _____ during the rail strike, with rail services being either delayed or canceled.

_____ 4. The ceiling of the study is _____ to leak when it rains. You'd better get it repaired.

_____ 5. The minority groups are usually excluded from the _____ of the society, which makes them feel alienated.

III. Guided Translation （寫出完整字彙）

1. 當 Zoe 發現兒子對她撒謊時，她無法克制自己不大發雷霆。

   Zoe couldn't r_____ herself f_____ flying into a rage when she found out her son had lied to her.

2. 有毒廢棄物必須小心處理。否則，它會汙染土壤和河川。

   Toxic waste must be d_____ o_____ very carefully. Otherwise, it will contaminate soil and rivers.

3. 鎮上的人已經被通知明起要停水。

   People in the town have been n_____ o_____ a water cut starting tomorrow.

4. 這些基金會被送往某些貧困國家，並將被用來幫助根除當地疾病。

   The funds are d_____ f_____ some poor countries and will be used to help eliminate local diseases.

5. 我強烈反對考試作弊。

I strongly d＿＿＿＿＿＿ o＿＿＿＿＿＿ cheating on exams.

NOTE

Round 2

I. Multiple Choice

(　　) 1. It is utterly ＿＿＿＿ to go hiking on such a stormy day.

       (A) absurd　　　(B) fiscal　　　(C) innumerable　(D) majestic

(　　) 2. One of the advantages of solar panels is that they require ＿＿＿＿ maintenance; rainwater alone is sufficient to wash the dust off the surface of the panels.

       (A) hearty　　　(B) pending　　　(C) ruthless　　(D) minimal

(　　) 3. The police were pinned down by a ＿＿＿＿ of bullets and had to request additional support.

       (A) lottery　　　(B) hail　　　(C) crossing　　(D) rail

(　　) 4. Mr. Yeats ＿＿＿＿ a complaint to the hotel regarding the foul smell coming from his bathroom.

       (A) lodged　　　(B) abbreviated　(C) nagged　　(D) puffed

(　　) 5. Lidia ＿＿＿＿ a bag of cookies and intended to snack on them after dinner.

       (A) shuttled　　　(B) resented　　(C) purchased　(D) flunked

(　　) 6. Martial law has long been ＿＿＿＿ in Taiwan. Now Taiwanese people have complete freedom.

       (A) counseled　(B) abolished　(C) surged　　(D) underlined

(　　) 7. The mother ＿＿＿＿ the baby's attention with a teddy bear as he started to cry.

       (A) defaulted　(B) disrupted　(C) defected　(D) diverted

(　　) 8. Hundreds of banks and financial institutions collapsed during the economic _____.

(A) emission　　(B) prospect　　(C) slump　　(D) transaction

(　　) 9. Cher has a large _____ with a variety of clothing, ranging from elegant evening dresses to heavy cashmere sweaters.

(A) intellect　　(B) wardrobe　　(C) layer　　(D) ranch

(　　) 10. When Tom questioned why he wasn't informed about the change of plan, his colleague _____ that it was because he didn't ask.

(A) presided　　(B) retorted　　(C) prolonged　　(D) rejoiced

(　　) 11. _____ can be opened to let in light or closed to keep out the sun.

(A) Stacks　　(B) Bolts　　(C) Liners　　(D) Shutters

(　　) 12. _____ and immediate measures must be taken to stop the disease from spreading.

(A) Descriptive　　(B) Drastic　　(C) Disastrous　　(D) Downward

(　　) 13. Tea and sugar were among the profitable _____ of Taiwan in the 19th century.

(A) boxers　　(B) comets　　(C) staples　　(D) checkups

(　　) 14. A furry rug on the smooth and shiny wooden floor creates an interesting _____ contrast.

(A) textile　　(B) texture　　(C) terrace　　(D) therapy

(　　) 15. Winona _____ a kidney to her father to save him from kidney failure.

(A) sponsored　　(B) racked　　(C) donated　　(D) vacuumed

II. Fill In the Blank （從下方選出適合字彙做適當變化，填入答案）

accustom	auction	entitle	excess	rotation

_____ 1. Some of the ancient coins being _____ are still in good condition and are worth tens of thousands of dollars.

_____ 2. As a senior member of the club, you are _____ to use all the facilities free of charge.

_____ 3. Our son's tuition is in _____ of what we can afford. We have to take out a loan from the bank.

_____ 4. Benedict practices crop _____ on the same field, alternating between growing sweet corn and wheat.

_____ 5. Having lived in Minnesota for five years, I have already become _____ to the cold winter here.

III. Guided Translation （寫出完整字彙）

1. 漁業活動、塑膠廢棄物和氣候變遷已對海洋生物造成嚴重影響。
Fishing activity, plastic waste, and climate change have had a serious impact on m_____ l_____.

2. 我要對我的演講做些修改，以增強它的說服力。
I am going to make m_____ t_____ my speech to enhance its persuasiveness.

3. 足球比賽的結果導致城市裡爆發暴動，憤怒的球迷砸毀了商店櫥窗並對汽車縱火。
The outcome of the football games s_____ a r_____ in the city, with angry fans smashing shop windows and setting cars on fire.

4. 我們送了 Jason 一本書以感謝他的協助。

We sent Jason a copy of the book i_____ a_____ of his

assistance.

5. 經濟仍舊每況愈下。看來政府無法阻止惡化的情況。

The economy is still in a d_____ s_____. It appears that

the government is unable to halt the worsening situation.

NOTE

Round 3

I. Multiple Choice

(   ) 1. If you feel tense in your neck, shoulders, or back, you can do some stretches to relieve _____ tension.

(A) solemn   (B) muscular   (C) ironic   (D) vigorous

(   ) 2. The scale of the mall is _____! It literally took me a whole day to explore the entire place.

(A) cellular   (B) aesthetic   (C) lunar   (D) massive

(   ) 3. When the Spanish first arrived in South America, they viewed the indigenous peoples there as _____ rather than civilized tribes.

(A) perils   (B) pastries   (C) savages   (D) servers

(   ) 4. Jay complimented his wife's new hairstyle in a(n) _____ tone. In reality, he found her hairstyle funny.

(A) mock   (B) serene   (C) ample   (D) perceptible

(   ) 5. The _____ rate of traffic accidents in Taiwan is one of the highest among developed countries.

(A) longitude   (B) occurrence   (C) mortality   (D) hospitality

(   ) 6. Keller spoke so _____ that the audience listened to him with close attention.

(A) feasibly   (B) anonymously

(C) mischievously   (D) eloquently

(   ) 7. Tana broke three records in the weightlifting competition at the Olympics and _____ herself once again.

(A) surpassed   (B) deemed   (C) stranded   (D) hampered

( ) 8. One of the great merits of this plan is its _____, which enables us to make adjustments when needed.
(A) acceleration   (B) corruption   (C) flexibility   (D) immunity

( ) 9. The decision to extend the duration of compulsory military service sparked considerable _____.
(A) fatigue   (B) controversy   (C) oppression   (D) detention

( ) 10. Reaching the summit of Mount Everest requires _____ and strength.
(A) enhancement   (B) enrichment
(C) enlightenment   (D) endurance

( ) 11. The decline of interest rates is expected to _____ the economy.
(A) deploy   (B) consent   (C) stimulate   (D) esteem

( ) 12. Local authorities failed to take immediate action to halt the spread of the _____.
(A) epidemic   (B) medication   (C) folklore   (D) equivalent

( ) 13. Don't be deceived by the empty _____ of politicians. They rarely keep their promises.
(A) nutrition   (B) rotation   (C) complement   (D) rhetoric

( ) 14. This piece of _____ furniture is characterized by its simple shape and bright color.
(A) stylish   (B) surplus   (C) agricultural   (D) chronic

( ) 15. When I visit a new settlement for the first time, I enjoy _____ the streets and getting acquainted with the surroundings.
(A) steering   (B) roaming   (C) reigning   (D) pinching

II. Fill In the Blank（從下方選出適合字彙做適當變化，填入答案）

flip	fume	seduce	session	unemployment

_____ 1. Boris _____ through the new book to see if any pages were torn, stained, or missing.

_____ 2. The press are not permitted to enter the courtroom when the court is in _____.

_____ 3. We all _____ at the bellboy who sent our luggage to the wrong room.

_____ 4. Teenagers may be _____ into smoking by tobacco advertisements that portray people as elegant and smart while smoking.

_____ 5. Government officials are attempting to address the _____ problems, but they are making no progress.

III. Guided Translation（寫出完整字彙）

1. 王國裡所有的子民都在為他們極為敬重的皇后的逝世哀悼。
   All the subjects of the kingdom were i_____ m_____ over the death of their highly respected queen.

2. 這座小鎮是一個知名的渡假勝地，以其溫和的天氣和平靜的鄉間景致著稱。
   This small town is a popular holiday resort, n_____ f_____ its mild weather and peaceful countryside view.

3. 在有些國家，價格標籤上的數字不包含營業稅。
   In some countries, the numbers on the price tags are e_____ o_____ sales tax.

4. Billy 年輕的時候交了一些壞朋友因而誤入歧途。

When Billy was young, he made some bad friends and w_____

a_____.

5. 我們謹代表學校當局對你在教學上的貢獻表達感謝。

O_____ b_____ of the school authorities, we would like

to express our gratitude for your dedication to teaching.

NOTE

Round 4

I. Multiple Choice

(   ) 1. The public were so _____ that they believed the politician would hold true to his word after being elected.

     (A) preventive   (B) melancholy   (C) irritable   (D) naive

(   ) 2. I am accustomed to spending time in the city library, _____ through all kinds of books and swimming in the sea of knowledge.

     (A) browsing   (B) thrusting   (C) striding   (D) compacting

(   ) 3. *Everything Everywhere All at Once* was _____ for eleven awards at the 95th Academy Awards.

     (A) nominated   (B) rifled   (C) marveled   (D) cited

(   ) 4. Despite his parents' objections, the _____ child insisted on sleeping with his pet dog.

     (A) subjective   (B) obstinate   (C) jolly   (D) monstrous

(   ) 5. The February 28 Incident was _____ by a clash between Taiwanese crowds and the Monopoly Bureau agents.

     (A) intrigued   (B) triggered   (C) unveiled   (D) staggered

(   ) 6. Shakespeare's plays demonstrate originality and his vast _____ of knowledge.

     (A) bass   (B) guideline   (C) breadth   (D) mentor

(   ) 7. The selection process relies on highly _____ tests. Those who are chosen must be exceptional.

     (A) oriental   (B) assertive   (C) rigorous   (D) coincident

(   ) 8. My passport is set to _____ in a month. I'll need to renew it as I have plans to travel out of the country in a couple of months.
(A) compile　　(B) depict　　(C) expire　　(D) kindle

(   ) 9. It wasn't until Richard turned ninety-eight that he began to lose his _____ .
(A) factions　　(B) faculties　　(C) formats　　(D) fragments

(   ) 10. E-commerce _____ has recently become widespread, leading to a growth in the number of people who have fallen victim to it.
(A) feminine　　(B) flake　　(C) fraud　　(D) forum

(   ) 11. The doctor _____ himself to help the sick people in the underdeveloped country.
(A) extracted　　(B) enrolled　　(C) exerted　　(D) endorsed

(   ) 12. I am sick of being _____ and underpaid, so I am going to quit.
(A) overdone　　(B) overworked　　(C) resided　　(D) repaid

(   ) 13. The conference room is _____ . It can accommodate five hundred people.
(A) shabby　　(B) dreadful　　(C) fireproof　　(D) spacious

(   ) 14. Sean was shattered when the doctor told him that his wife had _____ cancer. She didn't have much time left.
(A) captive　　(B) terminal　　(C) olive　　(D) imposing

(   ) 15. Being the only Taiwanese student in the university, Jessie had to find a way to _____ with the local community on her own.
(A) forge　　(B) diversify　　(C) integrate　　(D) subsidize

II. Fill In the Blank（從下方選出適合字彙做適當變化，填入答案）

gloom	glare	patch	slang	sober

_____ 1. If you consume too much alcoholic beverages and wish to _____ up, some would suggest drinking strong black coffee.

_____ 2. After a heated argument, it was hard for Nelly to _____ things up with Loran.

_____ 3. Stop _____ at me like that! You are well aware that you deserve the punishment.

_____ 4. The Wayne family was sunk in _____ after their family business went bankrupt.

_____ 5. Many parents and teachers struggle to comprehend the _____ used by teenagers nowadays.

III. Guided Translation（寫出完整字彙）

1. 這座微生物研究中心的周圍有保全每天二十四小時在巡邏。
   There are security guards o_____ p_____ around this microbiology research facility twenty-four hours a day.

2. Diane 看到 Jack 親吻另一名女孩後，於盛怒之下給了他一巴掌。
   Diane slapped Jack's face i_____ a f_____ after witnessing him kiss another girl.

3. 近期的研究闡明了這個疾病的來源，讓科學家離找出治療的方法又更進一步。
   Recent studies have s_____ l_____ on the origin of the disease, bringing scientists one step closer to finding a treatment.

4. 如果你發現自己被伴侶強迫做一些你不想做的事，試著維護自己的立場而不讓步。

If you find yourself being b_____ by your partner i_____

doing something you don't want to do, try to assert yourself and stand your

ground.

5. 當心山上變化莫測的天氣狀況。當天氣變糟時，找個安全的地方等待情況緩和。
不要繼續你的旅程。

B_____ o_____ the changing weather conditions in the

mountains. When it becomes rough, seek a safe spot and wait it out. Do not

continue your journey.

NOTE

Round 5

I. Multiple Choice

(   ) 1. In the recent #MeToo movement, many people have shared their experiences of sexual harassment and had their abusers _____ their wrongdoings.

(A) orient   (B) intervene   (C) script   (D) acknowledge

(   ) 2. Watson's love for railway is _____ in his extensive collection of train models.

(A) cosmetic   (B) airtight   (C) manifest   (D) weird

(   ) 3. The Christmas tree is decorated with silver and gold _____ .

(A) placements   (B) ornaments   (C) rods   (D) stimuli

(   ) 4. Some prisoners of war managed to _____ out of the prison camp in the middle of the night.

(A) sniff   (B) emigrate   (C) sneak   (D) bribe

(   ) 5. Playing online games is one of the most popular _____ among young people today.

(A) logos   (B) mansions   (C) pastimes   (D) orchards

(   ) 6. Poor road conditions pose a _____ to motorcyclists in Taiwan, with some sustaining serious injuries when they run over holes and fall off their bikes.

(A) purity   (B) dismay   (C) hazard   (D) morality

(   ) 7. Brian is _____ by the wealth and fame that he has recently attained.

(A) overwhelmed   (B) reproduced

(C) ribbed   (D) scrapped

( ) 8. The _____ of this facility is powered by dozens of windmills.
   (A) framework   (B) gathering   (C) freeway   (D) generator

( ) 9. Jemaine has been placed with a(n) _____ family. His biological parents, who had abused him, are not allowed to visit him.
   (A) oppressive   (B) selective   (C) initiative   (D) foster

( ) 10. Over fifty thousand fans _____ to secure tickets for the superstar's concert.
   (A) scrambled   (B) galloped   (C) pledged   (D) raided

( ) 11. Will's _____ in math is apparent. Despite being only thirteen, he can solve incredibly challenging problems.
   (A) prejudice   (B) endeavor   (C) vanity   (D) superiority

( ) 12. Lilian cannot resist the _____ of cakes, even though she is on a strict diet.
   (A) discrimination   (B) precaution
   (C) mandate   (D) temptation

( ) 13. Elvis joined the church _____ when he was a child. No wonder he can sing so beautifully.
   (A) monarch   (B) provision   (C) choir   (D) treaty

( ) 14. Light pollution has a substantial impact on our health, but many people are unaware of it and _____ the harm it causes.
   (A) underestimate   (B) uncover
   (C) undergo   (D) unlock

( ) 15. Poor management was _____ responsible for the trading company's financial loss.
   (A) partly   (B) pricelessly   (C) beneficially   (D) punctually

II. Fill In the Blank （從下方選出適合字彙做適當變化，填入答案）

grant	growl	peril	salt	salute

_____ 1. I've warned you about the danger of bungee jumping. If you insist on doing it, do it at your own _____.

_____ 2. Seeing the soldiers returning home from victory, people on the streets raised their hats in _____.

_____ 3. You should take the celebrity's words with a pinch of _____. He often tends to manipulate the media.

_____ 4. The impatient father _____ at his boy and told him to hurry up.

_____ 5. People who have never experienced a healthy relationship are inclined to take toxic traits in relationships for _____.

III. Guided Translation （寫出完整字彙）

1. 我被敲竹槓了！我跟攤販買的雷射筆在網路上只賣我買的半價。

   I've been r_____ o_____! The laser pen I bought from the street vendor only costs half of what I paid on the Internet.

2. 若沒有獲得明確同意，在任何情況下你都不應與他人進行肉體上的親密關係。

   Under no circumstances should you engage in physical intimacy with someone if you are not g_____ explicit c_____.

3. 車子如果每天在顛簸的路面上行駛很容易會故障。

   Cars can easily break down if they are driven on r_____ g_____ every day.

4. 獨自生活於大都市中，Baudelaire 有時會對週圍的人感到疏離。

   Living alone in the big city, Baudelaire sometimes feels a_____ f_____ the people around him.

5. 以往，已婚女子通常受限於家庭領域，生活圍繞著家庭和家務。

In the old days, married women were typically confined to the domestic sphere, where their lives r_____ a_____ family and household chores.

NOTE

Round 6

I. Multiple Choice

(　　) 1. No amount of money can _____ me to leave the job that I'm passionate about.

    (A) retail   (B) corrupt   (C) legitimate   (D) induce

(　　) 2. For most of the time, Calum enjoys being _____ rather than participating in gatherings and socializing.

    (A) solitary   (B) virgin   (C) customary   (D) bronze

(　　) 3. Fallon and Conan's business failed owing to the unfavorable economic climate, and they were _____ with a huge debt.

    (A) massaged   (B) quaked   (C) saddled   (D) softened

(　　) 4. A _____ high school is overseen by the city's department of education.

    (A) mortal   (B) suburban   (C) municipal   (D) civic

(　　) 5. Susie didn't want to _____ the task because she was afraid of the responsibility.

    (A) undertake   (B) swarm   (C) yearn   (D) soak

(　　) 6. Tires wear down because of _____ between the rubber and the road surface.

    (A) friction   (B) fleet   (C) fracture   (D) fluid

(　　) 7. Anyone interested in applying for the job should send their _____ to the human resources department by the end of June.

    (A) radius   (B) résumé   (C) reminder   (D) realm

( ) 8. When searching for a partner, some would focus more on whether that person is intellectually _____ with them.
(A) compatible   (B) bulky   (C) blonde   (D) alcoholic

( ) 9. Yellowstone National Park was the _____ of our trip to the US. The scenery there was simply magnificent!
(A) highlight   (B) intonation   (C) expiration   (D) rivalry

( ) 10. There is a great difference between the novel and its film _____. Nevertheless, both the novel and the film are considered successful.
(A) scope   (B) version   (C) scroll   (D) stimulation

( ) 11. Human beings should _____ nuclear power solely for the good of society.
(A) broil   (B) utilize   (C) refresh   (D) despise

( ) 12. Owing to the lack of any natural enemies, the alien species rapidly _____ this island.
(A) populated   (B) mowed   (C) reaped   (D) lightened

( ) 13. Buddhists from around the world assembled here to worship the _____ statue of Buddha.
(A) sacred   (B) orthodox   (C) envious   (D) patriotic

( ) 14. Scientists first _____ the idea of the atomic bomb in the 1930s. A decade later, it was put into practice.
(A) blurred   (B) detained   (C) scarred   (D) conceived

( ) 15. As the virus poses less of a threat, health authorities have made wearing a mask on public transportation _____.
(A) arithmetic   (B) compound   (C) optional   (D) provincial

II. Fill In the Blank（從下方選出適合字彙做適當變化，填入答案）

chair	hedge	plow	poke	rubbish

_____ 1. The secretary had been _____ around on the shelves for half an hour, trying to find an important document.

_____ 2. Many countries maintain robust armed forces as a _____ against any possible attacks.

_____ 3. Don't talk _____ ! What you said is completely incorrect!

_____ 4. We have no idea who will be in the _____ at tomorrow's meeting since our manager resigned abruptly a few days ago.

_____ 5. Donna's car _____ into a tree when she tried to avoid an oncoming truck.

III. Guided Translation（寫出完整字彙）

1. 當兩名走失的小孩被發現的時候，他們處在火車站的角落，緊緊依偎在一起。
   The two lost children c_____ t_____ each other in the corner of the train station when they were found.

2. Pearson 不符合跆拳道比賽的參賽資格，因為他未能達到體重規範。
   Pearson didn't q_____ f_____ the taekwondo competition because he failed to meet the weight requirement.

3. 你為何敵視性別運動呢？難道你不認為男生和女生都應該要從他們傳統的角色中獲得解放嗎？
   Why are you being h_____ t_____ gender movements? Don't you believe both men and women should be liberated from their traditional roles?

4. 當 Tracey 因毒品買賣而被逮捕時，他懇求大發慈悲。

When Tracey was arrested for drug dealing, he m_____ a

p_____ for mercy.

5. 冷風貫穿了 Davis 的毛衣，讓他瑟瑟發抖。

The cold wind p_____ t_____ Davis's sweater and made

him shiver.

NOTE

Round 7

I. Multiple Choice

(　　) 1. Chicken pox is a highly _____ disease, so if you have it, you will have to stay at home and self-isolate.

    (A) lucrative   (B) migrant   (C) fascinating   (D) infectious

(　　) 2. Why the _____ face? Is there anything wrong? Feel free to share if you'd like.

    (A) dental   (B) prior   (C) grim   (D) sloppy

(　　) 3. People in the past used to believe that the surface of the moon was smooth; they didn't know it's full of _____.

    (A) eclipses   (B) spheres   (C) nostrils   (D) craters

(　　) 4. We were impressed by the _____ works created by those imaginative artists.

    (A) implicit   (B) innovative   (C) courteous   (D) cardinal

(　　) 5. With the introduction of new AI language models, some argue that the _____ of AI reigning over humans is not far from realization.

    (A) nourishment   (B) prophecy   (C) molecule   (D) pilgrim

(　　) 6. As the monthly examination approaches, I _____ I will have to stay home the whole weekend studying for it.

    (A) allege   (B) reckon   (C) deafen   (D) incur

(　　) 7. The comedian's laughter was so _____ that the entire audience burst into laughter as well.

    (A) illusive   (B) interior   (C) chubby   (D) contagious

( ) 8. A police officer was discovered in _____ with local gangs to assist import and distribution of illegal substances.

(A) legacy   (B) hygiene   (C) league   (D) hierarchy

( ) 9. Before the plane crashed into the World Trade Center, many people saw it _____ over the New York skyline.

(A) scan   (B) bypass   (C) skim   (D) assess

( ) 10. Newborn babies need to receive various _____ to protect against illnesses and infections.

(A) injections   (B) implications   (C) illuminations   (D) intimacies

( ) 11. The newspaper features a(n) _____ of a successful local businessman every week.

(A) milestone   (B) profile   (C) installation   (D) ratio

( ) 12. Foreign teachers in Taiwan, regardless of their nationality, are paid in local _____.

(A) legislation   (B) currency   (C) mount   (D) nucleus

( ) 13. General Kenobi was skilled in _____. That was why his soldiers could defeat the enemy within a few of months.

(A) revivals   (B) transcripts   (C) tactics   (D) ordeals

( ) 14. Alex felt _____ when he was defeated by a robot in the chess game.

(A) humiliated   (B) hunched   (C) hurdled   (D) harassed

( ) 15. _____-packed food can be preserved for an extended period of time.

(A) Canvas   (B) Segment   (C) Cement   (D) Vacuum

II. Fill In the Blank（從下方選出適合字彙做適當變化，填入答案）

intent	convert	elevate	reminiscent	savage

_____ 1. Dawson is so _____ on finishing his research that he thinks of nothing else.

_____ 2. The retired steamboat was _____ to a floating restaurant, where people could enjoy their meals on the river.

_____ 3. The media made a(n) _____ attack on the governor's corruption and demanded his resignation.

_____ 4. Whenever Owen was feeling down, he turned to his favorite rock band. Their music never failed to _____ his spirits.

_____ 5. Several recent movies are _____ of the cinema of the US in the 1970s, not only in their plots but also in their styles.

III. Guided Translation（寫出完整字彙）

1. 記得出門放假時要關掉瓦斯供氣，做好預防。

   Always t_____ the p_____ of turning off your gas supply when you are away on vacation.

2. 這些瓷茶杯非常古老和脆弱。小心拿取它們。砸了你可負擔不起。

   These china teacups are old and fragile. Handle them w_____ c_____. You can't afford to drop them.

3. 基於同情，我跟坐輪椅的街頭小販買了一條口香糖。它有點貴，但只要我能幫助他，我就不會介意。

   O_____ of c_____, I bought a stick of gum from the street vendor in a wheelchair. It was a bit expensive, but that didn't bother me as long as I could help him.

4. 羅馬這座城市在人類歷史上位居要角，這就是為什麼它富有文化遺產。

Rome is a city that has played a prominent role throughout human history, which is why it is rich in c_____ h_____.

5. 有隻斑馬跟它的同伴們走散了，成為了獅群的獵物。

A zebra become separated from its companions and f_____ p_____ to a pride of lions.

NOTE

Round 8

I. Multiple Choice

(   ) 1. Since hotels are usually fully booked during the holidays, I _____ you make your reservations as early as possible.

    (A) recommend   (B) accord   (C) trifle   (D) revive

(   ) 2. So far, we haven't found anyone who possesses all the necessary _____ to fill the job.

    (A) nominations   (B) recommendations

    (C) manifestations   (D) qualifications

(   ) 3. It is impossible for a person to find inner peace while holding _____ against others.

    (A) optimism   (B) resentment   (C) applause   (D) patent

(   ) 4. The majority of the _____ in this community are senior citizens. People enjoy spending their retirement here.

    (A) modes   (B) playwrights   (C) refuges   (D) residents

(   ) 5. A good sportsperson shows respect for his or her _____, no matter how much he or she wishes to defeat them in the competition.

    (A) attorneys   (B) rivals   (C) mistresses   (D) outsiders

(   ) 6. Zack's honesty and _____ as a government official earned him the respect of everybody.

    (A) inventory   (B) integrity   (C) integration   (D) intervention

(   ) 7. I have always wanted to learn BASE jumping, but the thing is, I am _____ by heights.

    (A) liberated   (B) propelled   (C) obsessed   (D) intimidated

( ) 8. Jessica scolded her husband _____ because he didn't want to help with the kids.

(A) vaguely   (B) joyously   (C) radiantly   (D) indignantly

( ) 9. Elderly people are _____ to injury because their bodies are weakening.

(A) healthful   (B) valid   (C) liable   (D) invaluable

( ) 10. The level of digital _____ among young people today is very high. Almost everyone knows how to use a digital device.

(A) literacy   (B) landslide   (C) longevity   (D) liability

( ) 11. Vicky was seriously injured in a car crash and was immediately taken to a surgical _____.

(A) ward   (B) aisle   (C) compass   (D) specimen

( ) 12. A song in the public _____ can be used, remade, and distributed by anyone without any legal consequences.

(A) sector   (B) franchise   (C) housing   (D) domain

( ) 13. A(n) _____ has the capability of reaching a speed of twenty-seven thousand kilometers per hour, enabling it to escape gravity and enter outer space.

(A) airway   (B) amplifier   (C) spotlight   (D) spaceship

( ) 14. China had been engaged in _____ with Japan since 1937, which was two years before World War II broke out.

(A) bureaucrat   (B) scrutiny   (C) combat   (D) fascination

( ) 15. The total income from the competition, including broadcasting rights, _____, and ticket sales, approached one million dollars.

(A) doctrine   (B) likelihood   (C) refinement   (D) sponsorship

II. Fill In the Blank（從下方選出適合字彙做適當變化，填入答案）

ounce	presume	scrape	shred	smuggle

_____ 1. Ryan _____ a living as a stand-up comedian and managed to survive on a barely adequate income.

_____ 2. If Mr. White had a(n) _____ of common sense, he would not have invested all his money in the stock market.

_____ 3. Our office papers were torn to _____ before they were thrown away.

_____ 4. Before a person is found guilty, he or she is _____ innocent.

_____ 5. Several military personnel were caught _____ cigarettes into the country on a large scale.

III. Guided Translation（寫出完整字彙）

1. Teddy 真的很不會畫畫。他畫的所有房子和樹木都不成比例。

   Teddy is really poor at painting. All the houses and trees he drew were
   o_____ of p_____.

2. 自從 Timothy 被診斷罹癌之後，他的生活就備受折磨。但他仍想辦法找到力量，每天保持盼望。

   Ever since Timothy was diagnosed with cancer, his life has been
   i_____ t_____. Somehow, he still finds strength and remains hopeful every day.

3. 請教導我如何分辨真的和假的珍珠，這樣我才不會被騙。

   Please teach me how to d_____ b_____ real pearls and fake ones so that I don't get deceived.

4. 我不喜歡看恐怖片，因為每當出現突發驚嚇時，我總會被嚇個半死。

I don't enjoy watching horror movies because whenever there is a jump scare,

it always f＿＿＿＿＿＿ me o＿＿＿＿＿＿.

5. Logan 繼承父母留下的一大筆錢後，他就辭掉他的工作了。

After Logan f＿＿＿＿＿＿ h＿＿＿＿＿＿ to a large sum of money left

by his parents, he resigned from his job.

NOTE

Round 9

I. Multiple Choice

(   ) 1. Fung was _____ by one of the opponents in a football game, which rendered him unable to play anymore.

(A) lessened   (B) wearied   (C) squatted   (D) crippled

(   ) 2. Under the _____ of their instructors, the students loaded their rifles, took aim, and opened fire.

(A) precision   (B) supervision   (C) packet   (D) stature

(   ) 3. The family scandal had _____ a serious blow on the mayor's "Mr. Perfect" image.

(A) nourished   (B) inflicted   (C) rotated   (D) deprived

(   ) 4. The historic speech was _____ around the world via radio.

(A) relayed   (B) rioted   (C) rehearsed   (D) resumed

(   ) 5. Most Buddhist monks dedicate a significant amount of time to _____ as they believe it can help them gain insight into their religious beliefs.

(A) narration   (B) prescription   (C) obligation   (D) meditation

(   ) 6. In the past, students were prohibited from speaking _____ at school; otherwise, they would face punishment.

(A) directives   (B) dialects   (C) distinctions   (D) discourses

(   ) 7. It takes an expert to _____ an original from a copy.

(A) discriminate   (B) deplete   (C) discard   (D) detach

(   ) 8. Jason's _____ style of dressing sets him apart from the other boys.

(A) imperative   (B) collective   (C) extensive   (D) distinctive

(   ) 9. The government is making an effort to keep the old tradition from falling into _____ .
(A) doom   (B) density   (C) decay   (D) delegation

(   ) 10. Daniel and Eva were deeply _____ by their son's sudden death.
(A) distressed   (B) affirmed   (C) shielded   (D) plunged

(   ) 11. After several glasses of red wine, I experienced a _____ of dizziness.
(A) spectacle   (B) symphony   (C) sensation   (D) supplement

(   ) 12. Persistent _____ of emotions can cause mental health problems. We should express them when we feel the need.
(A) suppression   (B) exploitation
(C) junction   (D) correspondence

(   ) 13. Public opinion _____ toward peace. Most people do not favor war, but they'll defend themselves if necessary.
(A) tucks   (B) tilts   (C) distracts   (D) dedicates

(   ) 14. Animal fossils were once _____ but have transformed into stones after millions of years of natural processes.
(A) skeletons   (B) fractions   (C) trifles   (D) nudes

(   ) 15. Sophia _____ in computer science, and she works for a tech company that offers software design services.
(A) specializes   (B) reassures   (C) attains   (D) slashes

II. Fill In the Blank（從下方選出適合字彙做適當變化，填入答案）

accommodate	evolve	opt	resort	sly

_____ 1. Some people find it hard to _____ themselves to new jobs; it often takes them some time to become accustomed to a new environment.

_____ 2. A group of aggressive rebels _____ to terrorist acts to convey their anti-government stance.

_____ 3. Genetic evidence indicates that human beings _____ from apes.

_____ 4. Leo had been dating his secretary on the _____ for five years. The affair was finally exposed last week.

_____ 5. When faced with pressure, many men _____ to swallow it because they feel that seeking help is a sign of weakness.

III. Guided Translation（寫出完整字彙）

1. 哲學家陷入沉思，追尋生命的終極意義。
   The philosopher is deep in contemplation, i_____ q_____ of the ultimate meaning of life.

2. 我以為 Nick 對 Jess 的好感很明顯。為什麼只有我注意到？
   I thought Nick's a_____ f_____ Jess was apparent. Why was I the only person who had noticed it?

3. David 後悔在未審慎打聽的情況下就投資不熟悉的股票，最後導致他錢財盡失。
   David regretted that he invested in unfamiliar stocks without making d_____ i_____ and ended up losing all his money.

4. 沿海聚落的村民因為接到了海嘯警告，必須要撤離家園。

Villagers in the seaside settlements had to be e_____

f_____ their homes because they had received a tsunami warning.

5. 在 Margaret 接受工作之前，她考慮各種可能性，斟酌優點與缺點。

Before Margaret accepted the job, she p_____ o_____

the possibilities, considering the pros and cons.

NOTE

Round 10

I. Multiple Choice

(   ) 1. A leader with integrity would never _____ his or her power to satisfy personal desires.

       (A) abuse   (B) bound   (C) conduct   (D) spur

(   ) 2. In some states of the US, it is _____ for people to openly carry a gun in public.

       (A) monetary   (B) permissible   (C) orderly   (D) abrupt

(   ) 3. During the drought, the water levels in _____ throughout the country went down drastically.

       (A) peninsulas   (B) habitats   (C) cathedrals   (D) reservoirs

(   ) 4. Street vendors in this city are _____ for harassing tourists and selling fakes.

       (A) variable   (B) notorious   (C) upright   (D) decent

(   ) 5. Some politicians cannot be trusted as they frequently lie to the public and _____ the truth with rhetoric.

       (A) reinforce   (B) precede   (C) align   (D) obscure

(   ) 6. Mindy _____ her son affectionately when he returned home from his military duty.

       (A) scorned   (B) revolted   (C) sharpened   (D) embraced

(   ) 7. A(n) _____ is a book or a set of books that contains informative articles on various topics.

       (A) geometry   (B) index   (C) encyclopedia   (D) calligraphy

( ) 8. In spite of his best _____ , Larry was unable to swim against the current and was carried away by the river.

(A) eternity   (B) endeavors   (C) enrollment   (D) ethics

( ) 9. The premier _____ on the reasons why he believed it was unnecessary to build another nuclear power plant.

(A) escorted   (B) erected   (C) equated   (D) elaborated

( ) 10. Vice President Keller was _____ because his plot to overthrow the president was uncovered.

(A) exiled   (B) exceeded   (C) exclaimed   (D) excelled

( ) 11. Twelve-month-old babies must receive a measles _____ .

(A) vaccine   (B) asthma   (C) doze   (D) bonus

( ) 12. Viruses can become _____ through various means, so make sure to install anti-virus software on your computer.

(A) substantial   (B) component   (C) animate   (D) widespread

( ) 13. Elena suffered a series of _____ . Her father was injured in a car accident, her mother was diagnosed with cancer, and her son lost his job.

(A) appliances   (B) extensions   (C) clauses   (D) reversals

( ) 14. In my opinion, motorcyclists are very _____ . For most of them, the helmet is the only thing that can protect them.

(A) progressive   (B) vulnerable

(C) contemporary   (D) superficial

( ) 15. Christopher fractured his _____ when he fell from a horse ride. The accident left him paralyzed from the waist down.

(A) venue   (B) anchor   (C) brook   (D) spine

II. Fill In the Blank（從下方選出適合字彙做適當變化，填入答案）

alliance	facilitate	mentality	obscurity	stink

_____ 1. Mick's breath _____ of garlic and beer. I couldn't tolerate the smell at all!

_____ 2. Marge had dedicated her entire life to rural education in _____ until a news story made her an overnight celebrity.

_____ 3. Frank plunged into gambling as a result of his get-rich-quick _____, and pretty soon he became penniless.

_____ 4. The political and economic cooperation between Taiwan and the US has _____ a trend of studying abroad in the US.

_____ 5. Students felt betrayed when their teacher chose to be in _____ with the school authorities against them.

III. Guided Translation（寫出完整字彙）

1. 在審閱過這本書的手稿後，編輯決定書在出版前要做一些修改。
   After reviewing the book i_____ m_____, the editor concluded that some changes needed to be made before its publication.

2. 以防空武器強化防禦之後，陣地上的士兵等待著第二波攻擊。
   F_____ w_____ anti-aircraft weapons, soldiers at their positions awaited the second wave of attack.

3. 你到海邊游泳時要小心離岸流。這些海流會將你推離岸邊。
   You should be w_____ o_____ rip currents when you go swimming in the sea. They can push you away from the shore.

4. Charlotte 的遺產將會依照她的遺囑來做處理。
   Charlotte's remaining possessions shall be taken care of i_____ a_____ with her will.

5. 登上觀音山頂的時侯，淡水河以及綿延河岸的城市景緻讓我驚嘆。

When I reached the top of Mount Guanyin, I was filled w_____

a_____ by the view of the Tamsui River and the cities stretching

along the banks.

NOTE

Round 11

I. Multiple Choice

(　　) 1. One of the features of the air purifier is that it helps ＿＿＿ dust from the air.
(A) falter　　　(B) trim　　　(C) filter　　　(D) zoom

(　　) 2. Employers often provide bonuses as a(n) ＿＿＿ for workers to work harder and generate more profits to their companies.
(A) incentive　(B) pimple　　(C) endowment　(D) serving

(　　) 3. Soldiers must ＿＿＿ their commanding officer's orders without hesitation.
(A) execute　　(B) alter　　　(C) boost　　　(D) sustain

(　　) 4. We sat beneath a big tree with its leaves ＿＿＿ with its branches and completely blocking out the sun.
(A) purifying　(B) nurturing　(C) tripling　　(D) overlapping

(　　) 5. Phil's doctor has put him on a two-week course of ＿＿＿ to treat his infection.
(A) innovations　(B) nutrients　(C) antibiotics　(D) symptoms

(　　) 6. Rich people wore luxurious ＿＿＿ at the party to exhibit their wealth and status.
(A) outfits　　(B) warrants　(C) tokens　　(D) mattresses

(　　) 7. The Formosan black bear is an endangered species. If people do not take measures to protect them, they could go ＿＿＿.
(A) excessive　(B) exterior　(C) extinct　　(D) executive

(　　) 8. Students are encouraged to engage in ＿＿＿＿ activities, as it is believed to be able to help them develop their characters.

(A) constitutional (B) extracurricular

(C) residential (D) outgoing

(　　) 9. Alex never got married because he thought ＿＿＿＿ love could never be found in this ever-changing world.

(A) conceivable (B) tentative (C) eternal (D) cautious

(　　) 10. Health officials warn the public of an imminent flu ＿＿＿＿ this winter.

(A) outlook (B) outbreak (C) outing (D) outrage

(　　) 11. The spirit of my ancestors still runs through my ＿＿＿＿. I am as eager to explore the world as they once were.

(A) verticals (B) veins (C) vendors (D) vocals

(　　) 12. Having lived in the West for many years, the refugees still feel the ＿＿＿＿ from others from time to time.

(A) hostility (B) conquest (C) transplant (D) acquisition

(　　) 13. Nelson was killed ＿＿＿＿ with a stab to the heart amid the street fight.

(A) outright (B) thereby (C) awhile (D) overhead

(　　) 14. Nora ＿＿＿＿ not to speak to her best friend anymore after they had a fight.

(A) soared (B) mourned (C) vowed (D) bid

(　　) 15. Karl is a ＿＿＿＿ guy. Despite his desire to be liked and his eagerness to please everyone around him, he still lacks genuine friendships.

(A) crude (B) sentimental (C) pathetic (D) literal

II. Fill In the Blank （從下方選出適合字彙做適當變化，填入答案）

grill	hack	mortgage	oblige	surge

_____ 1. It took Roland twenty years of hard work to pay off the _____ on his house.

_____ 2. Having such a wonderful time at the party, I felt _____ to send a note of gratitude to my host and hostess.

_____ 3. Seeing the boy he liked accompanied by a good-looking guy, Arvin was consumed by a(n) _____ of jealousy.

_____ 4. Gary was _____ by the police about the hiding place of his associates for two days, and yet he still refused to talk.

_____ 5. Luther is wanted for _____ into several banks' computer systems and stealing a large amount of money.

III. Guided Translation （寫出完整字彙）

1. 要確保大部分的人口對特定疾病免疫，大規模疫苗接種便相當重要。
   Mass vaccination is imperative to ensure that the majority of the population becomes i_____ t_____ certain diseases.

2. 女王過世後，眾人列隊見她最後一面。
   Following the queen's death, people proceeded i_____ p_____ to pay their final respects to her.

3. 許多人存有當實況主或 YouTuber 賺錢很容易的幻覺。
   Many people are u_____ the i_____ that being a streamer or a YouTuber can make easy money.

4. 隨著颱風接近，人們預料到會有強降雨，便在家門口堆起沙包。
   As the typhoon approached, people stacked up sandbags by their doorways i_____ a_____ of heavy rainfall.

5. 因為預期這個小說家的新書會是另一部暢銷著作，許多人在出版前就已經訂購了一本。

O_____ the a_____ that the novelist's new book would be another hit, many people placed an order for a copy even before it was published.

NOTE

Round 12

I. Multiple Choice

(   ) 1. If you want the plants in your garden to _____, you need to enrich the soil.

(A) wither   (B) perish   (C) flourish   (D) shiver

(   ) 2. Preston searched _____ for his passport at the airport, with only an hour remaining before his flight departed.

(A) frantically   (B) robustly   (C) sneakily   (D) tactically

(   ) 3. In the intensive care units, _____ patients receive round-the-clock care.

(A) nasty   (B) feeble   (C) unanimous   (D) reckless

(   ) 4. _____ should double-check doctors' prescriptions to prevent any potential mistakes.

(A) Pharmacists   (B) Missionaries   (C) Prosecutors   (D) Referees

(   ) 5. Doctors warn that bad _____ can result in serious spine problems.

(A) recession   (B) migration   (C) posture   (D) outset

(   ) 6. The police officer instructed the witness to stop providing _____ details and to simply answer the questions asked.

(A) potent   (B) petty   (C) premier   (D) psychic

(   ) 7. We failed to notice the _____ in the vase when we bought it from the antique shop, and now it's too late to return it.

(A) foe   (B) fowl   (C) flaw   (D) foul

( ) 8. Each senior citizen over the age of seventy receives an old age _____ of NT$3,000.

(A) pension   (B) prototype   (C) proverb   (D) peasant

( ) 9. People in the town are _____ the shop because of the expired products it sells.

(A) advocating   (B) enhancing   (C) documenting   (D) boycotting

( ) 10. Our allies have not _____ us and are now coming to our aid. We shall withstand evil and prevail in the end.

(A) preached   (B) forsaken   (C) intruded   (D) provoked

( ) 11. All the rooms here are _____, so you don't need to share bathrooms and kitchens with others.

(A) pedestrians   (B) attics   (C) suites   (D) slums

( ) 12. Marvel Studios has collaborated with a number of brands and released a wide range of official _____.

(A) merchandise   (B) communism   (C) originality   (D) ambiguity

( ) 13. Your composition is clear and well-organized, but you should still avoid _____ mistakes such as typos.

(A) rebellious   (B) trivial   (C) insane   (D) intact

( ) 14. If you wish to _____ to first class, you will need to pay an additional fee.

(A) upgrade   (B) strap   (C) update   (D) tangle

( ) 15. Apollo 11, the space mission that first landed men on the surface of the Moon, unfolded in a _____ of publicity.

(A) sob   (B) backyard   (C) blaze   (D) coffin

II. Fill In the Blank（從下方選出適合字彙做適當變化，填入答案）

blunt	bosom	captive	inevitable	projection

_____ 1. You have to accept the _____ and be prepared to say farewell to your mom at any time.

_____ 2. Kennedy was assigned by his manager to make a profit _____ for the next quarter.

_____ 3. Tens of thousands of Allied _____ were freed from prison camps after the Germans surrendered unconditionally.

_____ 4. Upon arriving at their new home, the refugees were welcomed in the _____ of the local community.

_____ 5. You may not like to hear this, and yet, to be _____, you have not been doing a very good job recently.

III. Guided Translation（寫出完整字彙）

1. 這隻狗一定受到很好的照顧。你看！牠充滿了活力。

   The dog must be taken good care of. Look! It is f_____ of
   v_____ .

2. 這家科技公司處於破產邊緣。它的員工已經三個月沒領薪水了。

   The tech company is o_____ the b_____ of bankruptcy.
   Its employees have not been paid for three months.

3. 經過多年的武裝衝突，兩國最終達成停火協議。

   After years of armed conflicts, the two countries eventually r_____
   an a_____ to cease fire.

4. 關於部長的聲明你怎麼推論？這代表她同意教育改革嗎？

   What do you i_____ f_____ the minister's statement?
   Does it suggest that she agrees with the educational reform?

5. 學生拒絕服從學校的服儀規範，並在朝會上舉行抗議。

Students refused to c_____ t_____ the school's uniform

regulations and held a protest during the morning assembly.

NOTE

Round 13

I. Multiple Choice

(   ) 1. The police made some _____ inquiries before taking the suspect into custody.

(A) accountable   (B) preliminary   (C) reliant   (D) feasible

(   ) 2. Saoirse _____ over a log and fell to the ground when she was strolling in the woods.

(A) glided   (B) confronted   (C) stumbled   (D) rendered

(   ) 3. Madam President's contributions to world peace have brought great _____ to her country.

(A) storage   (B) bureaucracy   (C) prestige   (D) capability

(   ) 4. Rena was _____ from school for improper conduct.

(A) inherited   (B) suspended   (C) magnified   (D) tackled

(   ) 5. Several states in the US have passed laws to _____ smoking in public places.

(A) mobilize   (B) reconcile   (C) prohibit   (D) span

(   ) 6. Fabre _____ for air after chasing butterflies in the garden.

(A) gleamed   (B) grieved   (C) gasped   (D) generated

(   ) 7. In dreams, we are both the _____ and the explorer of the dream world because we construct and experience our dreams simultaneously.

(A) donor   (B) celebrity   (C) offspring   (D) architect

(   ) 8. What a(n) _____ wedding gown the bride is wearing. She looks glamorous!

(A) honorary   (B) ridiculous   (C) gorgeous   (D) virtual

(   ) 9. Becoming mature is a(n) _____ process. You can't expect to suddenly have everything figured out just because you've reached a certain age.

(A) miraculous   (B) recreational   (C) cumulative   (D) operational

(   ) 10. The embassy refused to _____ me an entry visa; therefore, I cannot reunite with my family.

(A) grant   (B) approximate   (C) compromise   (D) speculate

(   ) 11. You may know all the theory in the book, but it is no _____ for hands-on experience.

(A) sentiment   (B) compensation

(C) substitute   (D) boredom

(   ) 12. Sandra has a _____ knowledge of 20th-century Taiwanese literature.

(A) wholesale   (B) profound   (C) verbal   (D) radiant

(   ) 13. The landlord asked his _____ to leave because they had not paid their rent for three months.

(A) tenants   (B) trophies   (C) trustees   (D) thighs

(   ) 14. I feel that I have been discriminated against because of my gender and _____.

(A) splendor   (B) entity   (C) personnel   (D) citizenship

(   ) 15. It was a(n) _____ that the mudflow last night buried the whole village and killed everyone in it.

(A) exaggeration   (B) thriller   (C) casualty   (D) catastrophe

II. Fill In the Blank（從下方選出適合字彙做適當變化，填入答案）

irritate	phase	pipeline	slot	toll

_____ 1. The new currency is being _____ in to replace the old one.

_____ 2. Our new computer system is in the _____ and will be ready for operation next week.

_____ 3. Could you _____ one of Debussy's records into the CD player for me?

_____ 4. COVID lockdowns have taken a(n) _____ on students' academic performances and their ability to interact with others.

_____ 5. Ms. Chen got _____ by her students' mischievous behavior and decided to give them detention.

III. Guided Translation（寫出完整字彙）

1. Russell 的宗教信仰使他對性向與自己不同的人產生偏見。

   Russell's religious belief has b_____ him a_____ people whose sexuality is different from his.

2. 颱風離開後整個一片混亂。有傾倒的樹木、拋錨的汽車、被掀走的屋頂和淹水的道路。

   Everything was i_____ c_____ after the typhoon left. There were fallen trees, broken cars, blown-off roofs, and flooded roads.

3. 成為大人意味著認知到你的所想所求不是每次都能夠擺在他人的需求之前。

   Becoming an adult means learning that your desires cannot always take p_____ o_____ the needs of others.

4. 在現今人們為何對愛情越來越不確定這件事上，我獲得了有用的洞見。

I gained valuable i_____ i_____ the reasons why people nowadays are less and less certain about love.

5. 慈善演唱會在所有知名搖滾樂手齊聚臺上並演唱好幾首搖滾樂國歌的時候達到高潮。

The charity concert c_____ w_____ all the A-list rock and roll musicians coming together on stage and performing several rock anthems.

NOTE

Round 14

I. Multiple Choice

(   ) 1. The outcome of the election will remain unknown until the election
officials have counted all the _____ .
   (A) chestnuts   (B) ballots   (C) juries   (D) petitions

(   ) 2. Authorities _____ the public against visiting seaside attractions in
light of the approaching typhoon.
   (A) nickel   (B) caution   (C) mediate   (D) stroll

(   ) 3. Dominick has a seven-figure _____ annual income, which is why he
can afford a house in the city.
   (A) gay   (B) geographical   (C) gross   (D) gloomy

(   ) 4. Nothing can _____ for the time you have wasted; you had better
stop fooling around from now on.
   (A) compensate   (B) implement   (C) curb   (D) cater

(   ) 5. To strengthen the military forces, the government will _____ more
soldiers.
   (A) ratify   (B) rim   (C) recruit   (D) recite

(   ) 6. Oppressive _____ are, in reality, fearful of their people; they simply
hide their fear underneath all their cruel and dictatorial acts.
   (A) restraints   (B) rentals   (C) reptiles   (D) regimes

(   ) 7. Look! There are cattle _____ on the grass on both sides of the road.
   (A) grazing   (B) devouring   (C) preying   (D) stewing

(   ) 8. The _____ relay is a ritual in athletic meets. After it is lit, it will be passed around the country.
(A) torch　　　(B) torment　　　(C) tornado　　　(D) torrent

(   ) 9. As human-produced greenhouse gases increase, global warming intensifies because these gases would absorb solar _____.
(A) realization　(B) radiation　　(C) revelation　　(D) restoration

(   ) 10. _____ surround the cabin in the field, obscuring it from view.
(A) Glares　　　(B) Leases　　　(C) Batches　　　(D) Shrubs

(   ) 11. Heath Ledger's Joker is widely regarded as one of the most iconic movie _____ of all time.
(A) vetoes　　　(B) vouchers　　(C) ventures　　　(D) villains

(   ) 12. Government officials have _____ a comprehensive tax system reform in the hope of increasing revenues.
(A) enlightened　　　　　　(B) contemplated
(C) assassinated　　　　　　(D) deceived

(   ) 13. Gloomy economic prospects and worsening environmental conditions have created _____ circumstances for younger generations.
(A) adverse　　(B) vocational　(C) diplomatic　(D) coherent

(   ) 14. If you hate your job so much, leave and find a better one. It's no use just sitting there moaning and _____ all the time.
(A) groaning　　(B) blushing　　(C) straying　　(D) twinkling

(   ) 15. To everyone's surprise, the amateur team beat the professional team in the ice hockey _____.
(A) parliament　(B) tournament　(C) alternation　(D) corporation

II. Fill In the Blank （從下方選出適合字彙做適當變化，填入答案）

deter	interval	presumption	sequence	slam

_____ 1. All the regulations in this school are made on the _____ that human nature is inherently good.

_____ 2. MRT trains depart from the terminal stations at regular _____ from six a.m. to twelve a.m. every day.

_____ 3. When Simon sought help from Olivia, she _____ the door in his face.

_____ 4. We hope this new political alliance will _____ certain countries from making any reckless moves that could disrupt regional peace.

_____ 5. The system can only be activated in a specific _____, otherwise it will lock itself down.

III. Guided Translation （寫出完整字彙）

1. 我無法確切回答你的問題。你恐怕得去問別人。
   I can't answer your question w_____ c_____. I'm afraid you have to ask someone else.

2. 獲得充足睡眠、規律運動和維持均衡飲食能幫助你延長壽命。
   Getting enough sleep, exercising regularly, and maintaining a balanced diet help extend your l_____ s_____.

3. 對我來說，現代的畫作只是不同的顏色隨意揮灑在畫布上。我永遠無法真正了解它們的美學價值。
   To me, modern paintings are just different colors splashing on canvas a_____ r_____. I can never truly understand their aesthetics.

4. 當購物中心裡發現可疑的爆炸裝置時，防爆小組立刻接獲通報。

A b＿＿＿＿＿ s＿＿＿＿＿ was immediately called when a suspected explosive device was found in the shopping mall.

5. Janet 針對這個報告做了簡短的評論，接著便開放觀眾提問。

Janet delivered a brief c＿＿＿＿＿ o＿＿＿＿＿ the presentation and then proceeded to take questions from the audience.

NOTE

Round 15

I. Multiple Choice

(　　) 1. Sally's latest book pays _____ to her late grandfather, who was a war veteran.
(A) tribute　　　(B) criterion　　　(C) variation　　　(D) respondent

(　　) 2. Prolonged _____ has resulted in water and food shortages in the country, and its people are in desperate need of international aid.
(A) petroleum　　(B) duration　　(C) expenditure　(D) drought

(　　) 3. Dalton was one of the famous _____ in the American West, who had gunned down many of his opponents.
(A) outlaws　　(B) clusters　　(C) banquets　　(D) recipients

(　　) 4. Lady Spencer became a(n) _____ at a very young age. Her husband passed away a long time ago.
(A) widow　　　(B) apprentice　(C) clone　　　(D) scent

(　　) 5. Don't easily believe everything you read on the Internet. The information up there is not always _____ .
(A) tedious　　(B) inclusive　　(C) subtle　　　(D) credible

(　　) 6. For years, Penny has been _____ by the memory of the great flood that washed away her home.
(A) haunted　　(B) hailed　　　(C) handicapped　(D) harnessed

(　　) 7. The former prime minister's Alzheimer's became _____ when he began to lose his sense of time.
(A) supreme　　(B) comparative　(C) structural　　(D) noticeable

( ) 8. Eight Americans were held _____ by a terrorist group while traveling in West Asia.

(A) patron   (B) poultry   (C) hostage   (D) custody

( ) 9. President Cena _____ to public opinion and initiated a constitutional reform.

(A) condensed   (B) yielded   (C) trekked   (D) refuted

( ) 10. _____ to his elderly parents, William seldom keeps them company.

(A) Immense   (B) Imperial   (C) Indifferent   (D) Infinite

( ) 11. _____ of greetings vary from culture to culture, so we must be aware of the differences.

(A) Rituals   (B) Errands   (C) Arenas   (D) Utilities

( ) 12. An eagle _____ over the field, searching for rabbits and other small animals.

(A) shoves   (B) hovers   (C) beeps   (D) shuffles

( ) 13. Morty's dog _____ at the door, asking to be let out of the house.

(A) shrugged   (B) whined   (C) undermined   (D) evoked

( ) 14. Religions give people courage and teach them not to _____ even in the darkest of times.

(A) dissolve   (B) decline   (C) dwarf   (D) despair

( ) 15. The groom lifted the bride's _____ and kissed her during the wedding ceremony.

(A) maiden   (B) chore   (C) veil   (D) wig

II. Fill In the Blank（從下方選出適合字彙做適當變化，填入答案）

consultation	core	swamp	swap	ward

_____ 1. Wendy decided on her university major in _____ with her parents and teachers.

_____ 2. The boxer swiftly _____ off his component's blow and fought back.

_____ 3. I was shocked to the _____ when I heard such vicious language spoken by someone I highly respected.

_____ 4. Having spent all his summer vacation having fun, Patrick is now _____ with unfinished assignments.

_____ 5. Marianne asked Connell to _____ places with her so that she could talk to the attractive guy sitting next to him.

III. Guided Translation（寫出完整字彙）

1. Charlie 承諾 Samantha 會幫助她準備大學入學考試。
   Charlie has m_____ a c_____ to Samantha to assist her in preparing for the college entrance exam.

2. 當 Jane 發現 Peter 就是在晚上打擊罪犯的蒙面人時，她驚訝地看著他。
   Jane looked at Peter i_____ a_____ when she discovered that he was the masked man fighting criminals at night.

3. 臺灣在每年中秋節前後盛產柚子。
   Pomelos are i_____ a_____ in Taiwan every year around the Mid-Autumn Festival.

4. 在不久的過去，這個國家的女性仍被認為次於男性，並被稱作二等公民。

In the not-so-distant past, women in this country were still considered s ＿＿＿＿＿＿＿ t ＿＿＿＿＿＿＿ men and referred to as second-class citizens.

5. 為了增加追蹤人數，YouTuber 常會在影片結束前提醒觀眾去訂閱他們的頻道。

To boost the number of their followers, YouTubers often remind the viewers to s ＿＿＿＿＿＿＿ t ＿＿＿＿＿＿＿ their channels before they end the videos.

NOTE

Round 16

I. Multiple Choice

(　　) 1. Heaters are _____ during these chilly winter days.
- (A) comparable
- (B) barren
- (C) indispensable
- (D) hoarse

(　　) 2. The _____ of the scenery along the highway made our journey to the south rather boring.
- (A) clarity
- (B) fluency
- (C) presidency
- (D) monotony

(　　) 3. Jackson's good manners are _____ of the disciplined education he received in his childhood.
- (A) consecutive
- (B) reflective
- (C) narrative
- (D) legislative

(　　) 4. Moss climbed up the tree to _____ the kite that was stuck in the branches.
- (A) persevere
- (B) retrieve
- (C) squash
- (D) pedal

(　　) 5. I have a(n) _____ to make: It was I who ate all your sponge cake last night.
- (A) mechanism
- (B) confession
- (C) allergy
- (D) deficit

(　　) 6. Members of the opposition party condemned the expo as _____ from the ruling party.
- (A) prosecution
- (B) sovereignty
- (C) propaganda
- (D) reckoning

(　　) 7. The management made a(n) _____ to the labor union and agreed to give a pay raise.
- (A) intake
- (B) concession
- (C) corpse
- (D) trillion

(   ) 8. _____ crimes have been on the rise, prompting the city government to investigate why teens are driven to commit unlawful acts.

(A) Martial   (B) Judicial   (C) Neutral   (D) Juvenile

(   ) 9. It was Ridley's _____ that pushed everyone away from him. People just couldn't stand his ego.

(A) arrogance   (B) interpretation   (C) institution   (D) abortion

(   ) 10. Why did Lesley _____ at the station when she said she was going out of town?

(A) linger   (B) transmit   (C) foster   (D) cruise

(   ) 11. Recent studies have established a(n) _____ between excessive screen time and mental fatigue.

(A) lawsuit   (B) correlation   (C) equation   (D) transition

(   ) 12. Lowe felt as if the stiff collar of his shirt was literally _____ him. He could hardly breathe.

(A) soothing   (B) strangling   (C) staining   (D) shredding

(   ) 13. The lobby of the luxurious five-star hotel is decorated with a(n) _____ wall-to-wall carpet.

(A) lush   (B) crystal   (C) rear   (D) alien

(   ) 14. In *The Lord of the Rings*, even the powerful wizard dared not take the One Ring _____ he should be tempted by evil.

(A) likewise   (B) hence   (C) whereas   (D) lest

(   ) 15. Cobain played some _____ on the guitar to check if it was tuned.

(A) straits   (B) chords   (C) vowels   (D) audits

II. Fill In the Blank (從下方選出適合字彙做適當變化，填入答案)

aspire	incorporate	perspective	siege	tuition

_____ 1. Ever since she was little, Katherine has _____ to a career in space exploration.

_____ 2. Tim tried to _____ local elements into the design of the new city government building.

_____ 3. To put things in _____, so far there are no other alternatives except the one we have at hand.

_____ 4. College _____ in the US is notoriously expensive, so many students have no choice but to apply for student loans.

_____ 5. The press laid _____ to the hotel, waiting for the appearance of the superstar.

III. Guided Translation (寫出完整字彙)

1. 在等待班機的同時，你可以在候機室享用一些茶點。
   You can have some refreshments at the d_____ l_____ while waiting for your flight.

2. Dolan 感到一股衝動想牽起 Susan 的手，但他克制住了，因他不確定她對他的感情。
   Dolan felt an i_____ t_____ to hold Susan's hand but fought it down, for he was uncertain about her feelings toward him.

3. Karen 在恐怖的隨機殺人事件發生之後就避免搭乘捷運。
   Karen avoided taking the MRT s_____ t_____ the horrible random killing.

4. 所有的生物據信是來自誕生於三十億年前的有機體。

All living creatures are believed to d_____ f_____

organisms that were born three billion years ago.

5. 林務局官員雇用原住民獵人來協助做入侵種的移除。

Forestry Bureau hired indigenous hunters to assist in the r_____

o_____ invasive species.

NOTE

Round 17

I. Multiple Choice

(   ) 1. Some students were scolded by their teacher for _____ the accent of their new classmate who just returned from abroad.
   (A) certifying   (B) slaughtering   (C) overhearing   (D) mocking

(   ) 2. Customers choose us because we provide _____ service that is matched by none of our peers.
   (A) considerate   (B) poetic   (C) allergic   (D) exempt

(   ) 3. Scientists said that the _____ of this public health problem are beyond imagination.
   (A) dimensions   (B) diapers   (C) diameters   (D) directories

(   ) 4. Angie had a terrible experience of being cheated by her ex-boyfriend; therefore, it's only natural that she cannot _____ him.
   (A) excerpt   (B) gauge   (C) abide   (D) wrestle

(   ) 5. At a(n) _____ of 30,000 feet, the temperature outside the airplane is approximately minus 40 degrees Celsius.
   (A) attitude   (B) solitude   (C) institute   (D) altitude

(   ) 6. The police officer was asked to hand in his _____ and gun because he had violated the law enforcement procedures.
   (A) snatch   (B) badge   (C) pier   (D) lash

(   ) 7. There is a stain on your T-shirt. You should use _____ to wash it off.
   (A) bleach   (B) fabric   (C) sparkle   (D) velvet

(　　) 8. Ashley's son fell over in the playground and _____ his knee.

    (A) crammed　　(B) bruised　　(C) hardened　　(D) swayed

(　　) 9. In the past, sailors depended on the stars and compasses to _____ their ships.

    (A) modernize　　(B) civilize　　(C) navigate　　(D) publicize

(　　) 10. The whole village was _____ and destroyed by enemy bombers.

    (A) envisioned　　(B) blasted　　(C) stuttered　　(D) unified

(　　) 11. You must be _____ when explaining the rules to the students, or they won't understand.

    (A) explicit　　(B) ethical　　(C) exotic　　(D) external

(　　) 12. Warnings from the police only had a(n) _____ effect. Many were still fooled into taking illegal jobs in Cambodia.

    (A) marginal　　(B) polar　　(C) worthy　　(D) unprecedented

(　　) 13. During a war, the last thing a soldier should do is _____ his or her country.

    (A) erupt　　(B) adore　　(C) plead　　(D) betray

(　　) 14. Don't let your children put tiny toys or buttons in their mouths lest they should choke or _____.

    (A) snore　　(B) suffocate　　(C) thrill　　(D) haul

(　　) 15. _____ were built to turn the desert into a rich land on which people can grow crops.

    (A) Canals　　(B) Frontiers　　(C) Reefs　　(D) Probes

II. Fill In the Blank（從下方選出適合字彙做適當變化，填入答案）

agony	alternate	convict	particle	ripple

_____ 1. When Henley heard the bad news, he _____ between anger and desperation.

_____ 2. A(n) _____ of surprise spread through the conference room when the mayor announced that he would not be running for the next term.

_____ 3. Vincent was caught stealing things from the store again. He will be _____ of shoplifting for the second time.

_____ 4. The dictator was assassinated by a professional killer, and not a(n) _____ of evidence was left at the scene.

_____ 5. The victim of the car accident lay in _____ in the middle of the road awaiting the arrival of the ambulance.

III. Guided Translation（寫出完整字彙）

1. 這名醫師因對其病患性騷擾而被開除並受到起訴。

The physician was fired and then prosecuted for s_____ h_____ of his patients.

2. 人們在法庭上作證前需要宣誓自己的所言為真。

People have to t_____ an o_____ that they would tell the truth before they testify in court.

3. 市長喜歡去看棒球並非是因為他喜愛棒球，而是他喜歡與群眾交流。

The mayor likes to go to baseball games not so much because he likes baseball but because he likes to m_____ w_____ the crowd.

4. 如果我們的隊伍在奧運贏得冠軍，我們的國歌就會在我們被授予金牌時演奏。

If our team wins the championship at the Olympics, our n_____

a_____ will be played while we are awarded the gold medal.

5. 禁衛軍發動一場大型的攻擊以消滅占領城市外圍的叛軍。

The king's army l_____ a major a_____ to eliminate the

rebellious troops that had occupied the outskirts of the city.

NOTE

Round 18

I. Multiple Choice

(   ) 1. In our backyard stands a(n) _____ old oak tree, and we used to climb it all the time when we were kids.

      (A) edible   (B) disciplinary   (C) sturdy   (D) premature

(   ) 2. At the peak of the COVID-19 pandemic, tens of thousands of people were _____ to homes, hotel rooms, and hospital wards.

      (A) overflowed   (B) persisted   (C) injected   (D) confined

(   ) 3. Manson's hippie look has become his _____. He has long hair and always wears bell-bottom jeans.

      (A) lump   (B) disgrace   (C) trademark   (D) aviation

(   ) 4. Mandy looks _____ in that dark green velvet dress. She's definitely going to steal the show tonight.

      (A) fabulous   (B) fragrant   (C) finite   (D) forthcoming

(   ) 5. The old lady is very _____ to anyone who visits her. She would greet them with tea and biscuits.

      (A) glamorous   (B) hospitable   (C) graphic   (D) toxic

(   ) 6. Katie _____ a large doll in her arms, which was a birthday present from her father.

      (A) clasped   (B) enriched   (C) indulged   (D) ticked

(   ) 7. The Collins family moved into a new house in the suburbs within easy _____ distance of the city center.

      (A) reversing   (B) stunning   (C) transplanting (D) commuting

( ) 8. The pocketknife is a _____ tool that can be used as a screwdriver, a drill, a wine opener, and scissors.

(A) radical   (B) competent   (C) simultaneous (D) versatile

( ) 9. Critics of the new law _____ it as an assault on personal freedom.

(A) amended   (B) condemned   (C) inquired   (D) startled

( ) 10. The building exhibits the perfect _____, with its two halves matching in shape.

(A) scandal   (B) vertical   (C) stereotype   (D) symmetry

( ) 11. A group of police officers _____ the scene where the accident took place.

(A) comprised   (B) supervised   (C) prescribed   (D) collided

( ) 12. People have always wished for a utopia where love, peace, and equality _____, but reality often falls short of this ideal.

(A) rally   (B) testify   (C) conceal   (D) prevail

( ) 13. The stone wall on the hillside is a(n) _____ of an old castle from the 14th century.

(A) blot   (B) oasis   (C) relic   (D) myth

( ) 14. Do you know who will represent our country as the _____ to APEC this year?

(A) merger   (B) patriot   (C) delegate   (D) traitor

( ) 15. While it is convenient to use _____ to do the dishes, it is important to note that many of them are harmful to the environment.

(A) detergents   (B) jockeys   (C) sergeants   (D) banners

II. Fill In the Blank（從下方選出適合字彙做適當變化，填入答案）

brace	indigenous	merge	synthetic	vomit

_____ 1. The humming of bees _____ with the chirping of birds and forms a beautiful symphony of nature.

_____ 2. The dress is made of _____ fibers, so that it can be washed in the washing machine.

_____ 3. The revolting smell made Derek _____ up the food he had eaten.

_____ 4. The Maori language is the _____ language spoken by the native inhabitants in New Zealand.

_____ 5. As the plane prepared to make an emergency landing on the water, the flight attendants instructed all the passengers to _____ themselves for impact.

III. Guided Translation（寫出完整字彙）

1. 科學家將粒子的運動和光線的移動做類比。

   Scientists drew an a_____ b_____ the way a particle moves and the way light travels.

2. 在日據時代，殖民政府擁有許多商品的專賣權，像是菸草和酒精。

   During the Japanese colonial era, the colonial government had the m_____ o_____ many goods, such as tobacco and alcohol.

3. 荷爾蒙平衡如果受到擾亂，可能會導致不適，甚至是嚴重的健康問題。

   H_____ b_____, when disturbed, may cause discomfort and even serious health problems.

4. NTNU 是國立臺灣師範大學的縮寫。

NTNU is the a_____ f_____ National Taiwan Normal University.

5. 這位前主席的言論表露了她對黨內多數同志的輕蔑。

The former chairperson's remarks displayed her c_____ f_____ most of her comrades.

NOTE

Round 19

I. Multiple Choice

(   ) 1. When taking the _____, people usually stand on the right side so that those who are in a hurry can move along the left side.
(A) portfolio   (B) genre   (C) escalator   (D) fable

(   ) 2. The enemy may _____ our troops, but our morale is higher than theirs.
(A) utter   (B) withhold   (C) commission   (D) outnumber

(   ) 3. Kelly has a(n) _____ personality. She is confident in herself, and at the same time she is not afraid to admit her shortcomings.
(A) plural   (B) rigid   (C) transparent   (D) imminent

(   ) 4. Stephen King is a(n) _____ writer of thrillers. Some of his novels have been adapted for films.
(A) medieval   (B) nearsighted   (C) obscure   (D) renowned

(   ) 5. Scientists set off on a(n) _____ to the Antarctic to study the polar environment.
(A) abstraction   (B) shortage   (C) expedition   (D) plantation

(   ) 6. The famous badminton player defeated her opponent and secured her fourth _____ victory in women's singles.
(A) prospective   (B) symbolic   (C) successive   (D) indigenous

(   ) 7. Ineffective economic policies implemented by the government have _____ the decline of the manufacturing industry.
(A) depressed   (B) shattered   (C) accelerated   (D) banned

( ) 8. Hughes' superiors summoned him to a meeting to discuss his performance, and he attended _____.
(A) presumably　(B) accordingly　(C) theoretically　(D) viciously

( ) 9. The management should make the information more _____, so that all employees know what is going on in the company.
(A) enthusiastic　(B) accessible　(C) compulsory　(D) spontaneous

( ) 10. To enhance the credibility of the documentary on the Vietnam War, the film crew invited several veterans to _____ their stories.
(A) meditate　　(B) narrate　　(C) originate　　(D) radiate

( ) 11. With a deep passion for art, Mitch has steadily _____ an impressive collection of paintings and antiques over the years.
(A) fascinated　(B) consoled　(C) accumulated　(D) minimized

( ) 12. Bats have a keen sense of hearing, while dogs have an _____ sense of smell.
(A) eccentric　　(B) instinctive　(C) operative　　(D) acute

( ) 13. You will need considerable experience in _____ before you can run a company.
(A) administration　　　　(B) sovereignty
(C) fertility　　　　　　　(D) solidarity

( ) 14. The government has _____ NT$70 billion to the job creation program.
(A) illuminated　(B) attributed　(C) allocated　(D) schemed

( ) 15. Owing to its _____ geographical location, Taiwan serves as an economic and political center of East Asia.
(A) strategic　　(B) sole　　(C) spectacular　(D) stationary

II. Fill In the Blank（從下方選出適合字彙做適當變化，填入答案）

denial	pillar	prosecute	rip	stake

_____ 1. Several police officers were _____ for physically abusing their suspects.

_____ 2. Do not take too much pride in being a _____ of society, for with great power comes great responsibility.

_____ 3. Even though the danger of climate change hazards is very real, climate change _____ persists in many parts of the world.

_____ 4. The future of younger generations will be at _____ if we continue to turn a blind eye to the issue of extreme weather.

_____ 5. It _____ Edward's heart to see his son lying in bed and living on tubes.

III. Guided Translation（寫出完整字彙）

1. Lee 往往對他妻子犯的一點錯大驚小怪，讓她感到很惱怒。

   Lee tends to m_____ a f_____ about his wife's minor mistakes, and it really annoys her.

2. 別只會抱怨班上氣氛緊繃。你為何不做點什麼來改善呢？

   Don't just g_____ a_____ the tense atmosphere in your class. Why don't you do something to improve it?

3. 因為 Yoko 對海鮮過敏，她不能吃蝦，不然她會起疹子。

   As Yoko is allergic to seafood, she cannot eat shrimps or she will come out i_____ a r_____.

4. Alice 詢問教授這個故事是否可以視作性別平等的暗喻。

Alice asked the professor whether the story could be seen as a
m_____ f_____ gender equality.

5. 疲勞駕駛容易發生事故，因其應對交通狀況的能力已經下降了。

Drowsy drivers are p_____ t_____ accidents because
their ability to respond to traffic conditions has dropped.

NOTE

Round 20

I. Multiple Choice

(   ) 1. Michelle Yeoh is a(n) _____ movie star; she starred in numerous martial arts films not only in Hong Kong but also in Hollywood.

    (A) legendary   (B) cowardly   (C) outrageous   (D) inherent

(   ) 2. The government is planning to make a water _____ from the north to relieve the stress of water shortage in the south.

    (A) trauma   (B) diversion   (C) setback   (D) precedent

(   ) 3. When I boarded the plane, a flight attendant _____ me down the aisle to my seat.

    (A) ushered   (B) summoned   (C) conserved   (D) broadened

(   ) 4. Carson is a _____, as he publicly supports gender movements but privately makes discriminatory remarks about women.

    (A) victor   (B) hypocrite   (C) statesman   (D) saint

(   ) 5. A competent government should strive to ensure that every member of society is not _____.

    (A) excluded   (B) howled   (C) equalized   (D) hijacked

(   ) 6. Nowadays, you can find machines that _____ soap and toilet paper in almost every public toilet.

    (A) dispense   (B) vibrate   (C) salvage   (D) blaze

(   ) 7. It was Gibson's _____ to become the captain of his people and lead them to freedom.

    (A) ecology   (B) destiny   (C) stability   (D) cemetery

( ) 8. Andy quit his job because he could not tolerate his boss's _____ attitude anymore.

(A) arrogant　　(B) eligible　　(C) applicable　　(D) compassionate

( ) 9. Eugene's behavior has become very _____ ever since he got back from that summer camp. I wonder what happened to him there.

(A) elaborate　　(B) cognitive　　(C) abnormal　　(D) metropolitan

( ) 10. Japan's _____ attack on Pearl Harbor prompted the US to enter World War II.

(A) deliberate　　(B) anonymous　　(C) confidential　　(D) eloquent

( ) 11. Free holiday _____ are available at the information center over there.

(A) layouts　　(B) brochures　　(C) referendums　　(D) pitchers

( ) 12. It is good news that negotiators from two countries have accomplished a historic _____ in the arms control talks.

(A) breakup　　(B) crackdown　　(C) breakthrough　　(D) breakdown

( ) 13. Some birds have the ability to _____ the sounds in their surroundings.

(A) thrive　　(B) mimic　　(C) sympathize　　(D) paralyze

( ) 14. _____ form through the accumulation of snow, as the snow gradually compacts into enormous masses of ice.

(A) Chirps　　(B) Glaciers　　(C) Quivers　　(D) Bulks

( ) 15. The _____ under the photograph said, "Millions of people in the world still die of hunger every year."

(A) caption　　(B) irony　　(C) motto　　(D) quota

II. Fill In the Blank （從下方選出適合字彙做適當變化，填入答案）

compel	stabilize	theft	uprising	vapor

_____ 1. As the cause of the disease became known and more and more people got cured, the public health crisis has finally been _____.

_____ 2. Water _____ ascend to high altitudes and condense to form clouds, which then fall back to the ground as rain or snow.

_____ 3. Urban expansion has _____ wild animals to leave their habitats and learn to survive under the shadow of human civilization.

_____ 4. I was told that this neighborhood is not very safe. Numerous cases of _____ have been reported recently.

_____ 5. Faced with the popular _____, the dictator had no choice but to step down and go into exile.

III. Guided Translation （寫出完整字彙）

1. Lizzy 每個月都會捐出她一部分的薪水給幾個慈善組織，以幫助有需要的人。

Every month, Lizzy donates a portion of her salary to a couple of c_____ o_____ to help the people in need.

2. Harry 與他的母親有相似之處。人們總說他有他母親的眼睛。

Harry b_____ a r_____ to his mother. People always say that he has his mother's eyes.

3. 兩架飛機在數分鐘內撞入同一棟建築物絕非巧合。這是一場恐怖攻擊！

The fact that two planes crashed into the same building in a manner of minutes was n_____ c_____. It was a terrorist attack!

4. 對一個社群有益的東西可能對另一個社群是具破壞性的，因此並不存在一種能夠處理人類問題複雜性的通用方法。

What benefits one community can be d_____ t_____ another, so there is no one-size-fits-all approach to address the complexities of human issues.

5. 有些西歐國家已在尋找新的天然氣來源以切斷對俄羅斯的依賴。

Some West European countries have begun to look for new sources of gas to cut their r_____ o_____ Russia.

NOTE

Review 1

I. Multiple Choice

(　　) 1. It's already nine forty, but Olive still hasn't made _____ with us. There is a chance that she will be late again.
    (A) contact   (B) rust   (C) luck   (D) stress

(　　) 2. Driving personal vehicles is one of the contributing _____ to climate change because vehicles produce a lot of greenhouse gas.
    (A) hangers   (B) courts   (C) factors   (D) kits

(　　) 3. Our new president was _____ born. His parents come from a low socio-economic background.
    (A) instantly   (B) kindly   (C) humbly   (D) simply

(　　) 4. Working from home could be a good idea. Less time and money would be _____ on commuting.
    (A) stored   (B) wasted   (C) released   (D) carried

(　　) 5. I have an appointment with my _____. I need to get my hair trimmed.
    (A) lawyer   (B) accountant   (C) barber   (D) dentist

(　　) 6. Sharon is a very _____ person, and never hesitates to tell other people what she is thinking.
    (A) selfish   (B) direct   (C) graceful   (D) playful

(　　) 7. Rachel and I had a(n) _____ time at the picnic. We enjoyed the food and the scenery very much.
    (A) fresh   (B) open   (C) natural   (D) lovely

( ) 8. The government should take _____ measures to promote recycling in order to cut down on plastic waste.

(A) dumb   (B) military   (C) effective   (D) brief

( ) 9. I approached Mr. Roberts and greeted him, but he _____ me and walked away.

(A) dimmed   (B) braked   (C) shut   (D) ignored

( ) 10. Last night, the country was _____ by the strongest earthquake it had ever experienced in a century.

(A) struck   (B) defended   (C) licensed   (D) marked

( ) 11. Make sure you check the _____ forecast before going river tracing. A sudden shower can cause the water to rise really quickly.

(A) weather   (B) fortune   (C) election   (D) liquid

( ) 12. The helicopter crash on the outskirts of Taipei, which claimed the lives of several high-ranking officers, is the biggest news _____ today.

(A) influence   (B) item   (C) instance   (D) instrument

( ) 13. Volunteers on the street asked people to give _____ to charity to support those in need.

(A) generously   (B) honestly   (C) fluently   (D) wildly

( ) 14. _____ waiters and waitresses is customary in Western society.

(A) Taxing   (B) Topping   (C) Tipping   (D) Tying

( ) 15. When faced with potential danger, snails protect themselves by retreating into their _____.

(A) currents   (B) shells   (C) traces   (D) hives

II. Fill In the Blank（從下方選出適合字彙做適當變化，填入答案）

attach	being	butterfly	earth	weather

_____ 1. Where on _____ did you go? I've been searching for you all over the place.

_____ 2. Over the years, the rugged coast has been _____ by waves, gradually transforming into a marine platform.

_____ 3. I had _____ in my stomach when I saw the person I like coming toward me.

_____ 4. When submitting the application form, it is necessary to _____ a recent photo of yourself.

_____ 5. While I don't know exactly when dinosaurs came into _____, I do know that they went extinct around sixty-five million years ago.

III. Guided Translation（寫出完整字彙）

1. 在走出室外前，Sarah 的伴侶溫柔地把圍巾圍在她脖子上。

Before they went outside, Sarah's partner gently w_____ a scarf a_____ her neck.

2. 南非富含黃金與鑽石，這帶給該國相當可觀的稅收。

South Africa is r_____ i_____ gold and diamond, which has brought in significant revenues to the country.

3. 去購物之前先擬一張待買清單，這樣才不會漏買東西。

D_____ u_____ a list of the items that you need before go shopping so that you don't forget anything.

4. Lindsay 是我們目前最優秀的工程師。她能夠處理所有工作任務。

Lindsay is b＿＿＿＿＿＿ f＿＿＿＿＿＿ the best engineer we've got.

She is capable of handling all kinds of tasks.

5. 如果失業率持續攀升，我不知道這個國家會變得怎麼樣。

I don't know what will b＿＿＿＿＿＿ o＿＿＿＿＿＿ the country if the

unemployment rate keeps rising.

NOTE

Review 2

I. Multiple Choice

(   ) 1. The damaged kidney _____ a threat to the patient's health, so the surgeon had it removed and replaced it with a healthy one.
(A) quoted   (B) cured   (C) endured   (D) posed

(   ) 2. You should _____ sweets at the moment, or it will spoil your appetite for dinner.
(A) target   (B) couple   (C) hunt   (D) avoid

(   ) 3. There has been a certain _____ between my brother and me since our quarrel. We don't talk to each other anymore.
(A) advance   (B) conversation   (C) distance   (D) tunnel

(   ) 4. We had a lot of _____ with one of our customers who refused to pay, so we decided to take legal action.
(A) trouble   (B) honor   (C) expense   (D) creation

(   ) 5. The church was _____ fifty years ago, and it has been a vital part of the community ever since.
(A) found   (B) founded   (C) funded   (D) flooded

(   ) 6. When observing the stars, I always try to memorize their positions in _____ to each other.
(A) region   (B) result   (C) relation   (D) response

(   ) 7. It is a _____ that you couldn't join us for the movie tonight. I believe you would have enjoyed it.
(A) pleasure   (B) society   (C) shame   (D) trend

(　　) 8. _____ was served when that bunch of criminals were put behind bars.

    (A) Advice   (B) Justice   (C) Faith   (D) Honesty

(　　) 9. Students are required to conduct the experiment _____ . Teamwork or discussion with others is not allowed.

    (A) earnestly   (B) individually   (C) scientifically   (D) publicly

(　　) 10. Based on our data, we are _____ that next year's profits will be much higher.

    (A) terrific   (B) basic   (C) even   (D) confident

(　　) 11. I accidentally _____ my coffee, and it left a big black stain on my blouse.

    (A) stirred   (B) smiled   (C) spilled   (D) smelled

(　　) 12. For Joan, working as a secretary is a piece of cake, and she intends to look for a job that offers greater _____ .

    (A) pastes   (B) salaries   (C) challenges   (D) colas

(　　) 13. I try to live as economically as possible and not to _____ my parents with my living expenses.

    (A) fake   (B) burden   (C) engage   (D) rely

(　　) 14. Passengers on the _____ grew increasingly impatient as the train was already thirty minutes late.

    (A) platform   (B) ditch   (C) range   (D) package

(　　) 15. Jenny checked herself in the _____ before heading out for her date.

    (A) mask   (B) napkin   (C) pajamas   (D) mirror

II. Fill In the Blank（從下方選出適合字彙做適當變化，填入答案）

call	feed	nerve	pass	take

_____ 1. It's getting late, and I'm growing sleepy. Let's _____ it a day and go home now.

_____ 2. I won't stick around if Lola and Nelson are here. The way they show their intimacy really gets on my _____.

_____ 3. Vampire bats _____ on the blood of other animals.

_____ 4. I understand that you are busy right now, but this questionnaire will only _____ up a little of your time.

_____ 5. Elizabeth _____ out when she heard of her only son's death.

III. Guided Translation（寫出完整字彙）

1. Kent 總是在挑他員工的毛病，這便是為什麼公司裡所有人都不喜歡他。
   Kent is always f_____ f_____ with his employees, and that's why everyone in the office dislikes him.

2. 聖誕節就快到了，人們都忙著購買禮物和與親朋好友相聚。
   With Christmas just a_____ the c_____, people are busy shopping for presents and spending time with friends and family.

3. 緊急逃生門在公車行進時意外開啟，導致一名乘客跌出車外並喪命。
   The emergency exit door unexpectedly opened while the bus was i_____ m_____, causing a passenger to fall off and lost her life.

4. 在這間餐廳的店主過世後，她的獨子接管了生意。
   After the owner of the restaurant died, her only son t_____ o_____ her business.

5. 兩個族群之間的血腥衝突讓這個國家分崩離析。

The country is f_____ a_____ with bloody conflicts between the two ethnic groups.

NOTE

Review 3

I. Multiple Choice

(　　) 1. All the workers were feeling _____ because they had not received their wages for three months and were unable to reach their employers.

    (A) joyful   (B) frustrated   (C) casual   (D) armed

(　　) 2. I changed seats to get away from the man whose _____ smelled strongly of tobacco.

    (A) breath   (B) affair   (C) shed   (D) peak

(　　) 3. Memory, like everything else, _____ with age. Nothing is meant to last forever.

    (A) flocks   (B) flames   (C) folds   (D) fades

(　　) 4. The development of the new treatment is _____. It will fundamentally change the way we treat cancer.

    (A) revolting   (B) revolutionary   (C) outrageous   (D) envious

(　　) 5. Government officials have _____ that the price of petroleum will go up next week because of the ongoing war between Ukraine and Russia.

    (A) fastened   (B) announced   (C) complained   (D) requested

(　　) 6. It was a _____ that Preble fell from a five-story height and didn't get hurt at all.

    (A) norm   (B) miracle   (C) settlement   (D) plea

(　　) 7. Clerks are trained to _____ the bills for authenticity before accepting them.

    (A) expect   (B) inspect   (C) suspect   (D) prospect

(   ) 8. Stories of sexual harassment on the Internet have _____ memories of my own experience being harassed as a teenager.

(A) awakened   (B) buried   (C) merged   (D) invented

(   ) 9. Certain animals gather food before the end of summer to ensure they have _____ storage for the winter.

(A) sensible   (B) stubborn   (C) sincere   (D) sufficient

(   ) 10. I was swamped with so much information that my head started _____.

(A) spinning   (B) spitting   (C) setting   (D) sliding

(   ) 11. Jason can guess how people are feeling by _____ their body language.

(A) awaiting   (B) lifting   (C) observing   (D) interrupting

(   ) 12. Mr. Chu condemned his son's reckless _____ and said this could easily lead to conflicts.

(A) fictions   (B) errands   (C) deeds   (D) raises

(   ) 13. Switch to Channel 15 for me. The rock and roll charity concert is _____ live right now.

(A) debated   (B) broadcast   (C) adjusted   (D) forbidden

(   ) 14. Kelly's doctor prescribed her some _____ and instructed her to take one every six hours.

(A) pins   (B) pits   (C) pills   (D) piles

(   ) 15. All the students listened _____ to the guest lecturer, who had recently been awarded the Nobel Prize in Literature.

(A) respectfully   (B) respectably   (C) respectively   (D) relatively

II. Fill In the Blank（從下方選出適合字彙做適當變化，填入答案）

content	cunning	dispute	risk	tune

_____ 1. The military strongman, not _____ with overthrowing the current government, plans to invade neighboring countries.

_____ 2. Whether the educational reform should be initiated next year is still in _____.

_____ 3. Don't believe whatever Saul says. He is as _____ as a fox.

_____ 4. Dust, pollen, or animal hairs in the air can put people with allergies at _____.

_____ 5. Woods is poor at singing. He always sings out of _____.

III. Guided Translation（寫出完整字彙）

1. Shelby 被店員抓到在店內偷竊，隨後遭到警方逮補。

   Shelby was caught shoplifting by the clerk and was later placed u_____ a_____ by the police.

2. 這些士兵被捉為戰俘，他們的性命任由敵人擺布。

   Taken as prisoners of war, these soldiers' lives were a_____ the m_____ of their enemies.

3. 距我們大學畢業已經二十年了，我們決定來辦一場同學會。

   Twenty years after we graduated from college, we decided to have a c_____ r_____.

4. 有些父母會將照顧弟妹的責任強加在兄姊身上。

   Some parents would i_____ the responsibility of taking care of younger siblings u_____ the older ones.

5. 有些人相信基因改造可以增加作物的產值，而每個人都能夠因著這項科學發展獲得利益。

Some people believe genetic modification can enhance the crop production, and everybody will be p_____ f_____ this scientific advancement.

NOTE

Review 4

I. Multiple Choice

(　　) 1. Jimmy was accused of unlawful acts. To defend his reputation, he _____ with a strong statement and a lawsuit against his accusers.
   (A) evoked　　(B) countered　　(C) notified　　(D) strengthened

(　　) 2. All of the contestants anxiously awaited the _____ outcome. Nobody dared to say a word.
   (A) eventual　　(B) excessive　　(C) eternal　　(D) enormous

(　　) 3. We are optimistic about the _____ market for our new product. We believe it will sell well and generate substantial profits.
   (A) logical　　(B) practical　　(C) potential　　(D) medieval

(　　) 4. Brolin declined to make any comments _____ the recent election, as it is a highly sensitive topic.
   (A) regarding　　(B) minus　　(C) including　　(D) versus

(　　) 5. Bobby claims that he can tell my fortune by reading my _____ , but I think it is pure nonsense.
   (A) navy　　(B) palm　　(C) halt　　(D) lap

(　　) 6. My brother sliced a _____ of bread to make some sandwiches for me when I returned home from the baseball match.
   (A) cluster　　(B) mass　　(C) loaf　　(D) blouse

(　　) 7. Don't eat too many rice cakes at once. They cannot be easily _____ .
   (A) diagrammed　　(B) sunk　　(C) digested　　(D) flavored

(　　) 8. My teacher was not satisfied with my composition and asked me to ＿＿＿＿＿ it.

(A) register　　(B) revise　　(C) retreat　　(D) revenge

(　　) 9. Once everyone had taken their seats, the chairman ＿＿＿＿＿ to announce the objectives of the meeting.

(A) proceeded　　(B) preferred　　(C) peered　　(D) polished

(　　) 10. Rick felt very ill after consuming a ＿＿＿＿＿ mushroom and had to be sent to the hospital immediately.

(A) portable　　(B) passionate　　(C) previous　　(D) poisonous

(　　) 11. Remember to ＿＿＿＿＿ some salt and ground black pepper on the steak before grilling it.

(A) stagger　　(B) shiver　　(C) sprinkle　　(D) scoop

(　　) 12. Cecelia ＿＿＿＿＿ her voice and played a trick on me when she called me, but I could recognize it was her.

(A) disguised　　(B) enforced　　(C) revealed　　(D) dreaded

(　　) 13. Without a strong ＿＿＿＿＿, it is not easy for students to engage in active and independent learning.

(A) landmark　　(B) operation　　(C) motivation　　(D) intermediate

(　　) 14. Some psychologists believe in the concept of ＿＿＿＿＿ intelligences, suggesting that people can exhibit intelligence in different ways.

(A) moderate　　(B) misleading　　(C) miserable　　(D) multiple

(　　) 15. Our newly-designed tents come in ＿＿＿＿＿ shapes and sizes for you to choose from.

(A) various　　(B) single　　(C) rapid　　(D) dependent

II. Fill In the Blank（從下方選出適合字彙做適當變化，填入答案）

advantage	baggage	drain	hasty	partial

_____ 1. Many people's investments went down the _____ when the depression hit the country all of the sudden.

_____ 2. It would be to our _____ to advance now while the enemy's attack is falling apart.

_____ 3. Don't be _____ in judging a person. It takes time to fully know a person.

_____ 4. Make sure to claim your _____ before going through the customs at the airport.

_____ 5. Conan complains that his parents are _____ to his sister. He thinks they love her more than they love him.

III. Guided Translation（寫出完整字彙）

1. 在接到炸彈威脅後，警方加強巡邏並對任何可疑包裹保持高度警戒。

   After receiving a bomb threat, the police increased patrol and remained o_____ high a_____ for any suspicious packages.

2. 〈小星星〉是有名的搖籃曲，受到世代傳唱。

   "Twinkle, Twinkle, Little Star" is a popular n_____ r_____ that has been sung for generations.

3. 我的老師請我劃掉所有與文章主題不相關的的句子。

   My teacher asked me to cross out all the sentences that were not r_____ t_____ the article's topic.

4. 一般來說，青少年傾向反抗權威並堅持己見。

   In general, teenagers tend to r_____ a_____ authority and persist in their own ideas.

5. 調查的的回答通常有三種類別：「同意」、「不同意」和「沒意見」。

Survey responses generally f_____ into three c_____:

"Agree," "Disagree," and "No Comment."

NOTE

Review 5

I. Multiple Choice

(   ) 1. We need to hire a few more _____ to help with the shop during the high season.
    (A) assistants   (B) directors   (C) fighters   (D) losers

(   ) 2. At the end of the week, when George _____ all the good things that had happened to him in the past few days, he felt a sense of satisfaction.
    (A) recalled   (B) clarified   (C) deprived   (D) triggered

(   ) 3. My proposal was rejected because I couldn't _____ the directors that it was worth investing time and money.
    (A) manipulate   (B) convince   (C) disrupt   (D) multiply

(   ) 4. People often rush into a relationship with someone they've just met and _____ potential red flags.
    (A) overcome   (B) overlook   (C) overtake   (D) overthrow

(   ) 5. More and more people choose to live in cities to enjoy the convenience of _____ life.
    (A) underneath   (B) universal   (C) urgent   (D) urban

(   ) 6. Owing to the civil war, many refugees fled their country and have been living in _____ and poverty in remote refugee camps for several years.
    (A) isolation   (B) demonstration
    (C) significance   (D) combination

(   ) 7. In college, you don't need your professor's _____ to leave the classroom.

(A) mystery   (B) opportunity   (C) reaction   (D) permission

(   ) 8. The _____ body temperature of a human is around 35°C to 37°C.

(A) primary   (B) minor   (C) racial   (D) normal

(   ) 9. I like to read novels, watch YouTube, play the guitar, or go for a stroll during my _____ time.

(A) handle   (B) leisure   (C) local   (D) industry

(   ) 10. Unicorns are _____ creatures that exist only in legends and fantasies.

(A) imaginary   (B) immense   (C) imaginative   (D) imminent

(   ) 11. Jeans are made from a _____ textile known as denim, so they are not easily worn out.

(A) latest   (B) continual   (C) durable   (D) former

(   ) 12. My hands and face were _____ by sharp leaves as I passed through the bushes.

(A) scratched   (B) scorned   (C) scrambled   (D) scattered

(   ) 13. The kitchen smells _____ of coffee and it awakens my thirst for a cup of coffee.

(A) narrowly   (B) badly   (C) faintly   (D) formally

(   ) 14. Antarctica is a(n) _____ situated in the southernmost region of the Earth, where the land is mostly covered in ice.

(A) mainland   (B) desert   (C) ocean   (D) continent

(   ) 15. Norton makes a _____ of what is left of his allowance in the bank every week and has accumulated a considerable amount of savings over the years.

(A) mint   (B) property   (C) windshield   (D) deposit

II. Fill In the Blank（從下方選出適合字彙做適當變化，填入答案）

blink	creep	laundry	species	vacancy

_____ 1. The thief must have _____ into the house while I was asleep because I had no idea that my house got broken into.

_____ 2. An election will be held next week to fill the two _____ on the committee.

_____ 3. Before the washing machine was invented, people had to do the _____ using their bare hands.

_____ 4. When the light on the printer stops _____, it means the machine is ready for a new task.

_____ 5. Environmental activists urge that the government take action to protect the endangered _____.

III. Guided Translation（寫出完整字彙）

1. 這間餐廳藉由將整個空間點滿蠟燭來製造浪漫的氛圍。
   The restaurant creates a r_____ a_____ by lighting the entire room with candles.

2. 化石燃料被消耗殆盡是遲早的事。
   It is only a matter of time before f_____ f_____ are depleted.

3. 政府將建造一座紀念堂，以向救援行動中所有犧牲性命的英雄們致敬。
   The government is going to build a m_____ h_____ in honor of all the heroes who sacrificed their lives during the rescue operation.

4. 新的公路系統有助於提升南北之間的商品分配。
   New highway systems help improve the d_____ of g_____ between the north and the south.

5. 對教育改革持反對立場的人具有較為保守的態度。

   People who are against the educational reform have a more c_____

   a_____.

NOTE

Review 6

I. Multiple Choice

(　　) 1. After six weeks of parental leave, Sam is now ready to _____ his teaching job.

    (A) assume   (B) resume   (C) presume   (D) consume

(　　) 2. President Wazowski never expected that the leader of the private military company that he hired would become his _____ and threaten his regime.

    (A) patron   (B) refugee   (C) opponent   (D) missionary

(　　) 3. Even though it was apparent that Dike's troop stood no chance of winning, he _____ in telling his men to advance.

    (A) assisted   (B) resisted   (C) consisted   (D) persisted

(　　) 4. Cindy gave a(n) _____ grin as she was about to play a joke on her teacher.

    (A) progressive   (B) optimistic   (C) needy   (D) mischievous

(　　) 5. While Blake and Will were trying to climb over the fence, the sharp wires _____ their pants.

    (A) ripped   (B) zippered   (C) sipped   (D) dripped

(　　) 6. My house was a mess after the party. _____ bottles were scattered all over the place.

    (A) Discarded   (B) Strapped   (C) Refuted   (D) Blessed

(　　) 7. Don't give Chinese people a clock as a gift. It _____ death in Chinese culture.

    (A) preserves   (B) offends   (C) mentions   (D) symbolizes

(　　) 8. Being newly arrived in the country, Robin was unfamiliar with its customs, but by watching what the locals did and doing _____, he managed very well.

(A) namely　　(B) otherwise　　(C) meantime　　(D) likewise

(　　) 9. Holmes' opinion is heavily _____ by the false belief that women are incapable of rational thinking.

(A) prejudiced　　(B) privileged　　(C) prescribed　　(D) perceived

(　　) 10. Norman couldn't resist the _____ of country life and decided to move to Taitung.

(A) quakes　　(B) cramps　　(C) riots　　(D) lures

(　　) 11. Falling annual _____ have led to a cut in public spending.

(A) offerings　　　　　　　　(B) predecessors
(C) revenues　　　　　　　　(D) referees

(　　) 12. Climbing Mt. Everest was a real challenge, but the expedition team _____ and eventually reached the top.

(A) mobilized　　(B) persevered　　(C) protested　　(D) reigned

(　　) 13. Having turned against each other for years, the two neighbors were finally _____.

(A) overdone　　(B) motivated　　(C) reconciled　　(D) populated

(　　) 14. This case is referred to as the case of the century because its outcome will set a _____ for similar cases in the future.

(A) presidency　　(B) projection　　(C) propeller　　(D) precedent

(　　) 15. Logan held the smelling salts near Megan's _____ to bring her back to consciousness.

(A) lungs　　(B) nostrils　　(C) ribs　　(D) pimples

II. Fill In the Blank （從下方選出適合字彙做適當變化，填入答案）

compensation	rack	relay	thrive	stake

_____ 1. Billy's car was wrecked when the road suddenly opened up and swallowed it. He received NT$100,000 in _____ for his loss.

_____ 2. Employees have to work in _____ to make sure that the machines operate smoothly throughout the night.

_____ 3. I have already _____ my brains, but I still couldn't come up with any good idea.

_____ 4. Jane _____ on stress, but unlike her, I can't work under too much pressure.

_____ 5. The decision to send a rescue helicopter in the storm put the lives of the crew at _____ .

III. Guided Translation （寫出完整字彙）

1. Sebastian 展示了他理想城市的模型，裡頭有微縮尺寸的建築和道路。
   Sebastian displayed a model of his ideal city, featuring all the buildings and roads i_____ m_____ .

2. 我們應該理性看待我們的問題。雖然把計畫趕出來可能會失去一些品質，但我們必須做完才能得到學分。
   We should k_____ our problem in p_____ . While rushing our project may compromise some quality, we must complete it to get the credits.

3. 藥師在為處方籤配藥的時候必須非常謹慎，因為任何錯誤都可能造成致命的結果。
   Pharmacists must exercise extreme caution when f_____ a p_____ , as any mistake could result in a fatal outcome.

4. McCarthy 博士即將獲得醫學上的重大發現。他就快要找到愛滋病的治療方法。

Dr. McCarthy is o_____ the t_____ of a great discovery in medicine. He is about to find a treatment for AIDS.

5. Sherry 每天服用維他命補充品來增進健康。

Sherry takes daily v_____ s_____ to enhance her health.

NOTE

Review 7

I. Multiple Choice

(　　) 1. Heavy music was _____ through the loudspeakers during the show, and the audience was all very high.
   (A) amplified　　(B) diminished　　(C) forged　　(D) shielded

(　　) 2. Over the years, Dean has cultivated a(n) _____ relationship with each of his business partners.
   (A) tedious　　(B) geographical　(C) oriental　　(D) robust

(　　) 3. _____ headaches resulting from the stress disorder can last for several weeks.
   (A) Overall　　(B) Persistent　　(C) Perilous　　(D) Mortal

(　　) 4. A series of corruption _____ prompted the resignations of several high-ranking government officials.
   (A) slots　　(B) sculptures　　(C) saddles　　(D) scandals

(　　) 5. Carl and Carmen spent their holiday at a health _____, indulging in spa treatments, massages, and health food.
   (A) resort　　(B) landslide　　(C) pier　　(D) orchard

(　　) 6. My decision is not _____ at all. I had actually thought the whole thing through before I made up my mind.
   (A) reckless　　(B) dishonest　　(C) queer　　(D) rigid

(　　) 7. It _____ Brian to know that so many refugees drowned while attempting to cross the Mediterranean Sea.
   (A) ornaments　　(B) grieves　　(C) harms　　(D) deafens

(　　) 8. After a thirty-minute nap, I felt _____ and ready for the classes in the afternoon.

    (A) regretted   (B) refreshed   (C) replaced   (D) restricted

(　　) 9. Why don't you take a week off if you're feeling _____ from work?

    (A) suspended   (B) convicted   (C) fatigued   (D) dismayed

(　　) 10. Smith's sight started to _____ after driving for six hours straight, so he headed for a service area to get some rest.

    (A) wag   (B) sneeze   (C) oppress   (D) blur

(　　) 11. This old mechanical watch has _____ value for me. It was a gift from my late grandmother.

    (A) sentimental   (B) senior   (C) savage   (D) superficial

(　　) 12. Janet is extremely _____ , believing that whistling at night and pointing at the moon bring bad luck.

    (A) superstitious   (B) cautious   (C) enthusiastic   (D) dominant

(　　) 13. Our survey reveals that one in every four children is _____ at school, emphasizing the importance of teaching children respect and self-protection.

    (A) bullied   (B) discharged   (C) modified   (D) reproduced

(　　) 14. The newly-constructed _____ has a seating capacity of five thousand people and can be utilized for various kinds of artistic and cultural events.

    (A) aquarium   (B) boulevard   (C) auditorium   (D) pyramid

(　　) 15. School regulations that require students to _____ their shirts into their pants or skirts have become outdated and should be abolished.

    (A) tuck   (B) scroll   (C) pour   (D) cast

II. Fill In the Blank（從下方選出適合字彙做適當變化，填入答案）

brace	discriminate	rash	saddle	spur

_____ 1. Josh always does things on the _____ of the moment without prior planning.

_____ 2. Our country needs to _____ itself for water shortages as we enter the dry season.

_____ 3. We took pity on the new employee because she was _____ with the task of handling picky customers.

_____ 4. _____ against people based on race and sexuality is both disgraceful and illegal.

_____ 5. We have received a _____ of complaints about the worsening traffic condition in the past few weeks.

III. Guided Translation（寫出完整字彙）

1. 要想像沒有電力的生活是很困難的。我覺得沒有一個現代人能忍受。

It is difficult to c_____ o_____ life without electricity. I believe no modern person can tolerate it.

2. 時鐘停了。去拿一些新電池來換掉沒電的電池。

The clock has stopped ticking. Go have some new batteries to s_____ f_____ the dead ones.

3. 臺語有些字詞是來自從英語翻譯過來的日語。

Some words in Taiwanese are d_____ f_____ Japanese words translated from English.

4. Emily 無法克服失去寵物狗的情感創傷。她至今仍感到非常低落沮喪。

Emily has been unable to overcome the e_____ t_____ of losing her pet dog. She remains depressed and upset to this day.

5. 抗生素的濫用導致更強的細菌抗藥性，進而迫使用藥劑量增加。這形成了一個惡性循環。

The excessive use of antibiotics leads to increased bacterial resistance, compelling the need for higher doses of medication. It creates a v_____ c_____.

NOTE

Review 8

I. Multiple Choice

(   ) 1. It is truly a(n) _____ for Tina to be invited to give a lecture at the college department where she used to study.

       (A) fascination   (B) evaluation   (C) assessment   (D) compliment

(   ) 2. A group of drug dealers were arrested by the police just as they were about to _____ an illegal transaction.

       (A) fetch   (B) conduct   (C) ponder   (D) exchange

(   ) 3. Keisha's professor asked her to _____ on her understanding of the concept by providing concrete examples.

       (A) liberate   (B) elaborate   (C) alternate   (D) elevate

(   ) 4. A pack of hungry wolves chased down a deer and _____ it in mere minutes.

       (A) decayed   (B) distressed   (C) devoured   (D) disgusted

(   ) 5. Rumor has it that the abandoned mansion is _____ by the ghosts of its previous owners.

       (A) haunted   (B) mourned   (C) concealed   (D) betrayed

(   ) 6. Many law school students are upset about the way lawyers are _____ in a series of recent legal drama films.

       (A) scraped   (B) snatched   (C) sheltered   (D) stereotyped

(   ) 7. A racist is a person who harbors a _____ attitude toward people of different races.

       (A) ceramic   (B) sociable   (C) hostile   (D) noble

(　　) 8. Several parliament members were caught accepting bribes, which was met with a _____ of public criticism.

(A) trout (B) torment (C) torrent (D) token

(　　) 9. After two years of fighting, everyone was _____ of this meaningless war, yet there seemed to be no way of ending it.

(A) weary (B) weird (C) wicked (D) wary

(　　) 10. Pierce is caught in a _____ about whether to live with his parents or rent an apartment where he can enjoy his privacy.

(A) dimension (B) diagnosis (C) distraction (D) dilemma

(　　) 11. Hundreds of police laid _____ to the Legislation Yuan, keeping protesters from either getting in or out.

(A) stability (B) splendor (C) siege (D) succession

(　　) 12. Some of the most unique species on Earth are found _____ in Australia. They can be found nowhere else.

(A) arrogantly (B) symbolically (C) exclusively (D) indignantly

(　　) 13. Miraculously, the statue of the goddess remained _____ while everything else in the temple was reduced to ashes by the fire.

(A) insistent (B) intact (C) identical (D) innovative

(　　) 14. The two countries finally resumed _____ relations after years of opposition.

(A) diplomatic (B) equivalent (C) ironic (D) slight

(　　) 15. We didn't anticipate the _____ drop in temperature, so we didn't bring enough warm clothes.

(A) outgoing (B) abrupt (C) infinite (D) abundant

II. Fill In the Blank（從下方選出適合字彙做適當變化，填入答案）

diameter	dwell	exclude	grant	suspension

_____ 1. Russell knelt down and volunteered for the quest, and the king _____ his request.

_____ 2. Students should not be _____ from discussions of school affairs, as they are the main body of a school.

_____ 3. Could you enlarge the circle? I need one that is ten feet in _____.

_____ 4. Helen is afraid of walking on a(n) _____ bridge because she fears that she might fall over.

_____ 5. Stop _____ on past mistakes. What is done cannot be undone. It is time to look ahead now.

III. Guided Translation（寫出完整字彙）

1. 我哥哥每次遇到事情不如意的時候會有脾氣暴躁的傾向。他很容易感到惱怒。

   My brother is a _____ t _____ lose his temper whenever things don't go his way. He can easily get irritated.

2. 言語暴力經常會比肢體暴力造成更大的傷害。我們需要更多時間從言詞的傷害中恢復。

   V _____ a _____ can often do more harm than physical violence. It takes longer to heal from words that have wounded us.

3. 由於新的電腦程式與舊版的操作系統不相容，我建議你更新系統。

   Since new computer programs are not c _____ w _____ the old operating system, I suggest you update the system.

4. 紅十字會是一個非營利組織，致力於世界各地的災害救援。

The Red Cross is a n_____ o_____ committed to providing worldwide disaster relief assistance.

5. 愛撿便宜的人絕不會衝動消費。 相反的 ， 他們總是綜覽各處來尋找最便宜的商品。

Bargain hunters never buy o_____ i_____. Instead, they always look far and wide for the cheapest goods.

NOTE

PLUS 1

I. Multiple Choice

(   ) 1. David felt _____ by his overprotective parents and wished to leave home when he went to college.

    (A) tranquilized   (B) umpired   (C) smothered   (D) whirled

(   ) 2. Government officials cannot enact any laws without the _____ of the parliament.

    (A) sanction   (B) installment   (C) salvation   (D) ingenuity

(   ) 3. With the Internet, we can access hundreds of channels without using a(n) _____ .

    (A) sewer   (B) antenna   (C) tramp   (D) rustle

(   ) 4. Powerful winds and intense rainfall _____ houses and utility poles, causing tens of millions of dollars' worth of damage in just a few hours.

    (A) toppled   (B) rumbled   (C) peddled   (D) buckled

(   ) 5. Be sure to slow down while driving downhill along the _____ road, or you could easily fall off the side of the road.

    (A) brutish   (B) repressed   (C) dreary   (D) crooked

(   ) 6. As an ambitious woman, Margret doesn't _____ the prospect of giving up her career and becoming a housewife.

    (A) covet   (B) relish   (C) pluck   (D) ridicule

(   ) 7. During our visit to Bali, we spent almost every morning strolling through the _____ and exploring exotic goods.

    (A) blizzard   (B) braid   (C) bazaar   (D) barometer

( ) 8. The air feels refreshing after a light _____, and everything glows as the sky clears up.

(A) brooch   (B) drizzle   (C) enclosure   (D) hairdo

( ) 9. Zelda's father _____ her from studying abroad, saying that he couldn't afford it.

(A) distorted   (B) distrusted   (C) dissuaded   (D) dispatched

( ) 10. People look down on Samuel with a _____ because they don't think his way of achieving career success is legitimate.

(A) dosage   (B) pact   (C) sneer   (D) tremor

( ) 11. Stray dogs on the streets and in the parks can be a public _____. They may attack people, particularly young children.

(A) menace   (B) plight   (C) spire   (D) anecdote

( ) 12. Beachgoers _____ out on beach chairs, having their skin tanned under the sun.

(A) sprawl   (B) deteriorate   (C) brew   (D) grope

( ) 13. Lawrence's friends and family were really in _____ on hearing that he was granted the scholarship to visit UCLA.

(A) armor   (B) chatter   (C) ecstasy   (D) simmer

( ) 14. One of the major _____ to living in rural areas is the poor quality of public transportation.

(A) rites   (B) constituents   (C) heralds   (D) drawbacks

( ) 15. Food manufacturers should obey food safety regulations, which serve to _____ the health of customers.

(A) prick   (B) caress   (C) disregard   (D) safeguard

II. Fill In the Blank（從下方選出適合字彙做適當變化，填入答案）

fiddle	flutter	prop	streak	stunt

_____ 1. There is a _____ of absent-mindedness in Samson. He would respond when you talk to him, but you can feel that he's just not there.

_____ 2. Rina _____ her guitar on her thigh and played some folk tunes to entertain her guests.

_____ 3. Ethan kept _____ with his necktie when he was questioned by his superior about his work performance.

_____ 4. A famous actor was spotted climbing a building without any safety measures, and people questioned his motive for pulling a _____ like that.

_____ 5. Gordon has been in a _____ since his wife suddenly fell ill and was admitted to the surgical ward.

III. Guided Translation（寫出完整字彙）

1. 我犯了一個愚蠢的錯誤，我誤把 Alan 的女友叫成他前女友的名字了，搞得大家都很尷尬。

   I m_____ a b_____ by mistakenly calling Alan's girlfriend by his ex-girlfriend's name, and it embarrassed everyone.

2. 野柳地質公園以具有超現實感的海岸地景為特色，其中岩石受到海風和浪潮逐年風化。

   Yehliu Geopark features a surreal coastal landscape where rocks have been e_____ a_____ over time by sea winds and waves.

3. 藍調搖滾於六零年代開始風行。雖然藍調發源於美國，但卻是英國樂團率先使之成為風潮。

Blues rock c_____ i_____ v_____ in the 1960s. Although blues originated in the US, it was British bands that first popularized it.

4. 你媽媽對你不尊重人的態度很不滿。你最好去跟她道歉。

Your mother is d_____ w_____ your disrespectful attitude. You'd better apologize to her.

5. Neil 工作了一整天沒有進食，當他終於有時間坐下來吃東西時，他狼吞虎嚥地吃掉了他的潛艇堡。

Having been working all day without food, Neil g_____ u_____ his submarine sandwich when he finally had the chance to sit down and eat.

PLUS 2

I. Multiple Choice

(   ) 1. In some countries, people are permitted to use any means necessary, including deadly force, to engage anyone that _____ on their property.

    (A) embarks   (B) trespasses   (C) bogs   (D) stoops

(   ) 2. My grandmother appeared exhausted and _____ following her stomach surgery.

    (A) amiable   (B) frail   (C) pious   (D) emphatic

(   ) 3. You are going to make a(n) _____ of yourself if you keep nagging at others like this.

    (A) artery   (B) oar   (C) nuisance   (D) mouthpiece

(   ) 4. Aaron's _____ jokes about people's sexuality on the TV show were harshly criticized by the public.

    (A) vulgar   (B) triumphant   (C) bleak   (D) cosmopolitan

(   ) 5. Nixon told his men to get into position, and they waited for their rival gang to fall into their _____.

    (A) famine   (B) saloon   (C) flare   (D) snare

(   ) 6. In *Silent Spring*, author Rachel Carson cautioned readers about the negative effects on the environment caused by the excessive use of _____.

    (A) tempests   (B) poachers   (C) clans   (D) pesticides

(   ) 7. The Greeks _____ the city of Troy for years and had been unable to occupy it until they deceived the Trojans with the Trojan Horse.

    (A) besieged   (B) flicked   (C) incensed   (D) pecked

(   ) 8. A stranger _____ Ginny to follow him. She refused and immediately walked away.

    (A) conferred   (B) lamented   (C) beckoned   (D) stumped

(   ) 9. I could hear my father _____ as he watched his favorite comedy show.

    (A) chuckling   (B) migrating   (C) prefacing   (D) visualizing

(   ) 10. If you remove these _____ expressions, your essay will become much more readable.

    (A) redundant   (B) militant   (C) auxiliary   (D) thrifty

(   ) 11. Relations between the two countries were once _____, but now they have become enemies.

    (A) cordial   (B) incidental   (C) crunchy   (D) valiant

(   ) 12. Religion, in general, teaches people to forgive and not to _____.

    (A) whisk   (B) retaliate   (C) prune   (D) terminate

(   ) 13. When Britney heard the dance music, she couldn't resist swaying to its _____ beats.

    (A) stout   (B) mellow   (C) hysterical   (D) rhythmic

(   ) 14. _____ of teachers persists as a problem in some remote parts of the country, as most teachers are not willing to work there.

    (A) Enactment   (B) Materialism   (C) Deficiency   (D) Upbringing

(   ) 15. All of Nicholas' family members were killed in a _____ carried out by the Nazi regime.

    (A) substitution   (B) massacre

    (C) commemoration   (D) recurrence

II. Fill In the Blank（從下方選出適合字彙做適當變化，填入答案）

glisten	shudder	stammer	tariff	temperament

_____ 1. Elijah has a rather chilled _____. You can always feel at ease around him.

_____ 2. If we are not a member of the free trade entity, our exported goods will face _____ when entering its member countries.

_____ 3. People with a _____ in their childhood are often subject to ridicule by their peers and may thus become less self-confident.

_____ 4. Kilmer's body _____ with sweat while he was playing volleyball under the sun.

_____ 5. I _____ at the thought of what would happen if I failed to submit the assignment on time.

III. Guided Translation（寫出完整字彙）

1. 捷運列車突然煞車，Taylor 緊抓把手以保持平衡。
   As the MRT train braked abruptly, Taylor c_____ a_____ the handle to keep his balance.

2. 許多香港人嘗試尋求臺灣的政治庇護，但這些請求僅有部份獲得官方許可。
   Many Hong Kong people had tried to seek p_____ a_____ in Taiwan, but only a portion of these requests were granted by the authority.

3. 這一陣子我的心臟有時會突然抽痛。我覺得這是新冠疫苗的副作用。
   My heart sometimes t_____ w_____ sudden pain these days. I think it is a side effect of the COVID shot.

4. 不要一跑完一千六百公尺就馬上大口灌水。這會造成你身體很大的負擔。

Do not g_____ d_____ a large amount of water immediately after finishing a 1600-meter run. It puts your body under a lot of stress.

5. Getty 被一群綁匪擄走以要求勒金。然而，他有錢的爺爺卻拒絕付款。

Getty was h_____ for r_____ by a group of kidnappers. However, his wealthy grandfather refused to pay the money.

NOTE

學測英文混合題實戰演練

溫宥基　編著

新型學測 混合題 完全攻略
打造 最強解題 技巧

◆ 混合題閱讀策略大公開

全書共 14 單元，第 1 至 2 單元為「策略篇」，

介紹閱讀技巧及命題核心，

同步搭配應用練習，有效掌握閱讀策略與答題技巧。

◆ 訓練混合題型實戰能力

第 3 至 14 單元為「實戰篇」，

每單元一篇混合題題組，

題型含多選、填表、簡答、單詞填空、圖片配合題等，

精熟學測出題模式。

◆ 附文章中譯和詳盡解析

解析結合策略篇應試邏輯，進一步強化解題思維、

內化作答要點。

學測英文字彙力
6000 PLUS⁺ 隨身讀

三民英語編輯小組　彙整

第一本 完整收錄最新字表的隨身讀！
獨家贈送「拼讀」音檔，用聽的也能背單字！

本書特色

◆ **符合學測範圍！**

依據「高中英文參考詞彙表（111 學年度起適用）」編寫，收錄 Level 1－6 字彙及 PLUS 實力延伸字彙，共 250 回，掌握學測字彙，應戰各類考試。

◆ **拼讀音檔！**

專業外籍錄音員錄製，音檔採「拼讀」模式（success，s-u-c-c-e-s-s，success，成功），用聽覺輔助記憶。

◆ **補充詳盡！**

補充常用搭配詞、同反義字及片語，有利舉一反三、輕鬆延伸學習範圍。

國家圖書館出版品預行編目資料

30天計畫PLUS：打造進階英文字彙題本／丁雍嫻,邢
雯桂,盧思嘉,應惠蕙編著.－－初版一刷.－－臺北市：
三民，2023
面；　　公分.－－（英語Make Me High系列）

ISBN 978-957-14-7671-1　（平裝）
1. 英語 2. 詞彙

805.12　　　　　　　　　　　　　　112011676

英語 *Make Me High* 系列

30 天計畫 PLUS：打造進階英文字彙題本

編 著 者	丁雍嫻　邢雯桂　盧思嘉　應惠蕙
發 行 人	劉振強
出 版 者	三民書局股份有限公司
地　　址	臺北市復興北路 386 號 (復北門市)
	臺北市重慶南路一段 61 號 (重南門市)
電　　話	(02)25006600
網　　址	三民網路書店 https://www.sanmin.com.tw
出版日期	初版一刷 2023 年 9 月
書籍編號	S872520
I S B N	978-957-14-7671-1

108課綱、全民英檢中高級適用

英語 *Make Me High* 系列

30天計畫PLUS+：
打造 進階 英文字彙題本

丁雍嫻 邢雯桂 盧思嘉 應惠蕙 編著

解析本

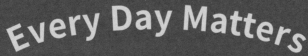

Every Day Matters
備戰 30 天
全面提升大考字彙力

6000+

三民書局

Table of Contents

練習完一個回次後，你可以在該回次的◯打勾並在 12/31 填寫完成日期。

Round 1

I. Multiple Choice

1. A	2. D	3. B	4. D	5. A
6. D	7. A	8. C	9. B	10. C
11. A	12. A	13. B	14. A	15. A

1. 如果你打算成為一位律師,你得學習講話不要含糊,並且清楚大聲地表達。
   (A) **含糊講話**;(B) 嘎嘎作響;(C) 呻吟;(D) 窺視

2. Fiona 總是遲到且從不認真工作。 我懷疑她會有升職的機會。
   (A) 迷信的;(B) 熱情的;(C) 憤慨的;(D) **懷疑的**

3. 因為 Boxton 被老闆視為公司的重要人才 ,所以獲得了提拔。
   (A) 中尉;(B) **資產**;(C) 管理員;(D) 地產

4. 秋葉在風中顫抖著。 它們看起來隨時都會飄落。
   (A) 使目眩;(B) 用槳划船;(C) 打碎;(D) **顫抖**

5. Bill 與他祕書外遇一事的揭發毀了他的政治生涯。
   (A) **揭發**;(B) 收益;(C) 評估;(D) 禁止

6. Jade 對批判社會理論非常精通。你寫作業遇到瓶頸的時候都可以向她尋求建議。
   (A) 值得尊敬的;(B) 顧問的;(C) 崇高的;(D) **博學的**

7. Jessie 在機場跟她的兒子說再見時,她哽咽了。
   (A) **腫塊 (哽咽)**;(B) 海綿;(C) 新手;(D) 哺乳動物

8. 得知這個老菸槍被診斷出肺癌並不是一件令人訝異的事。
   (A) 使分心;(B) 命令;(C) **診斷**;(D) 使傷殘

9. Susie 使用掃描機將一些相片掃進她的電腦裡。
   (A) 收銀員;(B) **掃描機**;(C) 研討會;(D) 優惠券

10. 這名老人一直陷在過往的好日子裡。他太常去想這些事了。
    (A) 察覺;(B) 使蒙羞;(C) **居住 (陷在)**;(D) 調整

11. 失去這些無價的珠寶讓店主感到非常沮喪。
    (A) **使沮喪**;(B) 規訓;(C) 切斷;(D) 排出

12. 在過去,中產階級女性往往穿著讓她們感到非常束縛的服裝。
    (A) **服裝**;(B) 涼鞋;(C) 行李箱;(D) 香水

13. 這棟高樓的價值未曾縮減,因它處於市中心的絕佳位置。
    (A) 體現;(B) **縮減**;(C) 充盈;(D)服從

14. 如今,越來越多人從事健身,希望能甩掉幾公斤。
    (A) **擺脫**;(B) 翻轉;(C) 修補;(D) 殺死

15. 這款工業用清潔劑能清潔又髒又油的磁磚,讓它們看起來跟新的一樣。
    (A) **磁磚**;(B) 珊瑚;(C) 事件;(D) 引信

II. Fill in the Blank

1. midst	2. abundant	3. turmoil
4. apt	5. mainstream	

1. 在疫情、氣候變遷和戰爭當中,人們的生活飽受壓力。★ in the midst of 在…之中

2. 這座島上富有稀有熱帶植物,是為它的特色之一。★ abundant 豐富的

3. 鐵路運輸在鐵路罷工期間一片混亂,火車班次不是延遲就是取消。
   ★ in (a) turmoil 處於混亂狀態

4. 書房的天花板下雨時容易漏水。你最好去把它修一修。★ be apt to 有…傾向的

5. 少數群體通常被排除於社會主流之外,使得他們覺得自己受到疏離。★ mainstream 主流

III. Guided Translation

1. restrain; from
2. disposed; of
3. notified; of
4. destined; for
5. disapprove; of

Round 2

I. Multiple Choice

1. A	2. D	3. B	4. A	5. C
6. B	7. D	8. C	9. B	10. B
11. D	12. B	13. C	14. B	15. C

1. 在這種暴風雨的日子去健行真的是很荒謬。
   (A) **荒謬的**；(B) 財政的；(C) 無數的；(D) 雄偉的

2. 太陽能板的其中一項優點是它們需要極少的維護；單單雨水就足以洗去面板上的灰塵。
   (A) 誠摯的；(B) 未定的；(C) 殘忍的；(D) **極少的**

3. 警方被一陣彈雨所壓制，得請求額外支援。
   (A) 彩券；(B) **一陣**；(C) 路口；(D) 鐵路

4. Yeats 先生針對從他浴室飄出的臭味向飯店提出投訴。
   (A) **提出**；(B) 縮寫；(C) 嘮叨；(D) 噴出

5. Lidia 買了一袋餅乾，並打算晚餐後拿它們當點心吃。
   (A) 往返；(B) 憎恨；(C) **購買**；(D) 考不及格

6. 戒嚴令在臺灣早已廢止。臺灣人民現在享有完全的自由。
   (A) 建議；(B) **廢止**；(C) 湧現；(D) 強調

7. 媽媽在嬰兒開始哭的時候以泰迪熊轉移他的注意。
   (A) 拖欠；(B) 擾亂；(C) 叛離；(D) **轉移**

8. 數百家的銀行和金融機構在經濟蕭條期間倒閉。
   (A) 排放；(B) 前景；(C) **蕭條**；(D) 交易

9. Cher 有一個收納多樣服飾的大衣櫥，從優雅的晚禮服到厚重的喀什米爾毛衣都有。
   (A) 智力；(B) **衣櫥**；(C) 階層；(D) 牧場

10. 當 Tom 質問為何他沒收到計畫改變的通知，他的同事反駁說是他自己沒問。
    (A) 主持；(B) **反駁**；(C) 延長；(D) 高興

11. 遮板可以打開讓光線進來或關閉以阻擋陽光。
    (A) 一堆；(B) 門閂；(C) 郵輪；(D) **遮板**

12. 必須要採取嚴厲且立即的措施才能阻止疾病擴散。
    (A) 描述的；(B) **嚴厲的**；(C) 災難性的；(D) 向下的

13. 茶和糖是十九世紀臺灣其中兩項具獲利能力的主要產物。
    (A) 拳擊手；(B) 彗星；(C) **主要產物**；(D) 健康檢查

14. 在光滑的木地板上擺著一張絨毛的地毯形成了有趣的質地對比。
    (A) 紡織品；(B) **質地**；(C) 露臺；(D) 治療

15. Winona 捐了一顆腎臟給她父親 ，使他免於腎衰竭之苦。
    (A) 贊助；(B) 折磨；(C) **捐獻**；(D) 用吸塵器清掃

II. Fill in the Blank

1. auctioned	2. entitled	3. excess
4. rotation	5. accustomed	

1. 有些在拍賣會上的古錢幣仍跟新的一樣，並值上萬元。★ auction 拍賣

2. 作為俱樂部的資深成員，你擁有免費使用所有設施的權利。★ entitle sb to V 使有權做…

3. 我們兒子的學費超越了我們所能負擔的。我們得要向銀行貸款。★ in excess of 超過 (額度)

4. Benedict 在同一塊地上實施輪作，交替種植甜玉米和小麥。★ rotation 輪流

5. 在明尼蘇達州住了五年後，我已經習慣了這裡的冷冬。★ become accustomed to 習慣於…

III. Guided Translation

1. marine; life
2. modifications; to
3. sparked; riot
4. in; acknowledgement
5. downward; spiral

Round 3

I. Multiple Choice

1. B	2. D	3. C	4. A	5. C
6. D	7. A	8. C	9. B	10. D
11. C	12. A	13. D	14. A	15. B

1. 如果你覺得頸部、肩膀或背部有點緊繃，你可以做一些伸展來舒緩肌肉壓力。
   (A) 莊嚴的；**(B) 肌肉的**；(C) 諷刺的；(D) 活力充沛的

2. 這間購物中心的規模很大！我真的花了一整天才逛完整個地方。
   (A) 手機相關的；(B) 美學的；(C) 月球的；**(D) 巨大的**

3. 當西班牙人剛抵達南美洲時，他們視當地的原住民族為野蠻人而非文明部落。
   (A) 危險；(B) 油酥糕點；**(C) 野蠻人**；(D) 伺服器

4. Jay 以一種假裝的語氣稱讚他妻子的新髮型。事實上，他覺得她的髮型很滑稽。
   (A) 假裝的；(B) 平靜的；(C) 足夠的；(D) 可察覺的

5. 臺灣交通事故的死亡率在已開發國家中名列前茅。
   (A) 經度；(B) 發生的事；**(C) 死亡數量**；(D) 好客

6. Keller 說得頗有說服力以至於聽眾都專注地聆聽他的話。
   (A) 可行地；(B) 匿名地；(C) 頑皮地；**(D) 具說服力地**

7. Tana 在奧運舉重比賽上打破了三項紀錄，並再度自我超越。
   (A) 超越；(B) 認為；(C) 使陷於困境；(D) 阻礙

8. 這項計畫其中一個非常好的優點是彈性，這讓我們能夠在需要時作調整。
   (A) 加速；(B) 貪汙腐敗；**(C) 彈性**；(D) 免疫

9. 延長兵役長度的決定產生了許多爭議。
   (A) 疲憊；**(B) 爭議**；(C) 壓迫；(D) 羈押

10. 攻頂聖母峰需要耐力及體力。
    (A) 提升；(B) 豐富；(C) 啟發；**(D) 耐力**

11. 利率的降低預期能刺激經濟。
    (A) 部署；(B) 同意；**(C) 刺激**；(D) 尊敬

12. 地方當局未能採取立即行動來阻止疫情擴散。
    (A) 疫情；(B) 藥物；(C) 民間傳說；(D) 同等事物

13. 別被政治人物空洞的華美言詞給欺騙了。他們鮮少遵守承諾。
    (A) 營養；(B) 旋轉；(C) 讚美；**(D) 華美言詞**

14. 形式簡約和色彩明亮是這件時尚傢俱的特色。
    (A) 時尚的；(B) 剩餘的；(C) 農業的；(D) 慢性的

15. 當我第一次拜訪新聚落時，我喜歡漫步在街上以熟悉環境。
    (A) 駕駛；**(B) 漫步**；(C) 統治；(D) 擠捏

II. Fill in the Blank

1. flipped	2. session	3. fumed
4. seduced	5. unemployment	

1. Boris 快速翻過這本新書來檢查是否有任何破損、髒汙或缺頁。★ flip through sth 快速翻閱

2. 法院開庭時媒體不允許進入法庭內。
   ★ in session 在會期間

3. 我們都對把我們的行李送錯房間的門僮感到生氣。★ fume at sb 對…發怒

4. 青少年可能會受到菸草廣告的引誘而去抽菸，廣告中的人在吸菸的時候看起來優雅又聰明。
   ★ seduce sb (into) V-ing 引誘某人做某事

5. 政府官員試圖解決失業問題，但他們毫無進展。★ unemployment 失業 (率)

III. Guided Translation

1. in; mourning
2. notable; for
3. exclusive; of
4. went; astray
5. On; behalf

Round 4

I. Multiple Choice

1. D	2. A	3. A	4. B	5. B
6. C	7. C	8. C	9. B	10. C
11. C	12. B	13. D	14. B	15. C

1. 大眾相信這名政治人物當選後會兌現他的話實在很天真。
   (A) 預防的；(B) 憂鬱的；(C) 易怒的；**(D) 天真的**

2. 我習慣待在市立圖書館裡翻閱各種書籍，徜徉於知識的海洋。
   (A) 翻閱；(B) 猛推；(C) 邁步；(D) 壓縮

3. 《媽的多重宇宙》在第九十五屆奧斯卡金像獎中受到十一項提名。
   (A) 提名；(B) 迅速翻找；(C) 對…驚嘆；(D) 引用

4. 儘管父母反對，倔強的小孩堅持和他的寵物狗一起入睡。
   (A) 主觀的；**(B) 固執的**；(C) 愉快的；(D) 駭人的

5. 二二八事件因著臺灣民眾和專賣局查緝員的衝突而引發。
   (A) 激發好奇；**(B) 引發**；(C) 發表；(D) 蹣跚

6. 莎士比亞的戲劇展現了獨創性與他知識的淵博。
   (A) 低音；(B) 指導方針；**(C) 廣度**；(D) 指導者

7. 遴選過程建立在極為嚴格的測試之上。被選中的人必定非常優秀。
   (A) 東方的；(B) 自信的；**(C) 嚴格的**；(D) 同時發生的

8. 我的護照一個月後就要到期。我得要辦理更新，因為我計畫幾個月後要出國。
   (A) 彙編；(B) 描繪；**(C) 到期**；(D) 點燃

9. Richard 到了九十八歲之後身體機能才開始下降。
   (A) 派系；**(B) 機能**；(C) 安排；(D) 碎片

10. 電商詐騙在近期變得氾濫，導致受害者人數上升。
    (A) 女性；(B) 小薄片；**(C) 詐騙**；(D) 網路論壇

11. 這名醫生盡力幫助這個低度開發國家的病人。
    (A) 提取；(B) 登記；**(C) 運用**；(D) 贊同

12. 我受夠了過勞又低薪，所以我要辭職。
    (A) 過度；**(B) 過度工作**；(C) 居住；(D) 報答

13. 會議室很寬敞。它可以容納五百人。
    (A) 破舊的；(B) 討厭的；(C) 防火的；**(D) 寬敞的**

14. Sean 聽到醫生說他的妻子患了末期癌症時非常崩潰。她時間不多了。
    (A) 被俘的；**(B) 末期的**；(C) 橄欖綠的；(D) 宏偉的

15. 作為大學裡唯一的臺灣學生，Jessie 得自己想辦法融入當地社群。
    (A) 偽造；(B) 使多樣化；**(C) 融入**；(D) 補助

II. Fill in the Blank

1. sober	2. patch	3. glaring
4. gloom	5. slang	

1. 如果你喝了太多酒精飲料而想要醒酒，有人建議喝濃的黑咖啡。★ sober up 醒酒

2. 在一場激烈的爭執後，Nelly 很難與 Loran 和好了。★ patch things up with sb 和某人重修舊好

3. 不要再這樣瞪我了！你很清楚你應該受到懲罰。★ glare at 怒視…

4. Wayne 家族在他們的家族事業破產後陷入了慘淡。★ gloom 憂鬱

5. 許多父母和老師很難理解現今青少年使用的俚語。★ slang 俚語

III. Guided Translation

1. on; patrol
2. in; fury
3. shed; light
4. bullied; into
5. Beware; of

Round 5

I. Multiple Choice

1. D	2. C	3. B	4. C	5. C
6. C	7. A	8. D	9. D	10. A
11. D	12. D	13. C	14. A	15. A

1. 在近期的 #MeToo 運動中，許多人分享了他們受性騷擾的經驗，並讓加害者承認他們的錯誤。
   (A) 使適應；(B) 干涉；(C) 寫劇本；**(D) 承認**

2. Watson 對鐵道的熱愛顯見於他大量的火車模型收藏。
   (A) 美容的；(B) 密閉的；**(C) 顯而易見的**；(D) 怪異的

3. 聖誕樹上裝飾著金銀相間的裝飾品。
   (A) 臨時工作；**(B) 裝飾品**；(C) 釣竿；(D) 刺激

4. 一些戰俘趁著深夜的時候潛逃出了戰俘營。
   (A) 嗅聞；(B) 移居他國；**(C) 偷偷溜走**；(D) 行賄

5. 玩線上遊戲是最受時下年輕人歡迎的消遣之一。
   (A) 商標；(B) 豪宅；**(C) 消遣**；(D) 果園

6. 惡劣的路況對臺灣的摩托車騎士造成危害。有些在騎過坑洞時因此跌倒受重傷。
   (A) 純潔；(B) 驚慌；**(C) 危害物**；(D) 道德觀

7. Brian 對於他近期獲得的財富與名聲感到不知所措。
   (A) 使不知所措；(B) 重現；(C) 揶揄；(D) 放棄

8. 這座設施的發電機是由許多風車驅動。
   (A) 架構；(B) 聚會；(C) 高速公路；**(D) 發電機**

9. Jemaine 已被安置在寄養家庭裡。虐待他的親生父母不被允許去探望他。
   (A) 壓迫的；(B) 選擇(性)的；(C) 開始的；**(D) 寄養的**

10. 超過五萬名粉絲爭搶超級巨星演唱會的門票。
    (A) 爭搶；(B) 飛奔；(C) 發誓；(D) 突襲

11. Will 在數學上的優越是顯而易見的。儘管他才十三歲，他卻能夠解非常困難的題目。
    (A) 偏見；(B) 努力；(C) 虛榮；**(D) 優越**

12. Lilian 無法抗拒蛋糕的誘惑，即便她正在進行嚴格的節食。
    (A) 歧視；(B) 預防措施；(C) 授權；**(D) 誘惑**

13. Elvis 小時候有加入教會的合唱團。難怪他唱歌如此動聽。
    (A) 君主；(B) 準備；**(C) 合唱團**；(D) 條約

14. 光害對我們的健康有很大的影響，但很多人沒有意識到這點，並低估它造成的危害。
    (A) 低估；(B) 揭露；(C) 經歷；(D) 打開門鎖

15. 管理不善是造成這間貿易公司財務虧損的部分原因。
    (A) 部分地；(B) 無價地；(C) 有益地；(D) 準時地

II. Fill in the Blank

1. peril	2. salute	3. salt
4. growled	5. granted	

1. 我已經警告你高空彈跳的危險。如果你堅持要去，那麼風險自負。
   ★ do sth at one's (own) peril 從事…風險自負

2. 看到士兵們勝利歸鄉，街道上的人們舉帽致敬。★ in salute 致敬

3. 你應該對那位名人的話抱持存疑。他經常傾向操弄媒體。
   ★ take sth with a pinch of salt 對…存疑

4. 不耐煩的父親對著他的兒子咆哮，要他動作快一點。★ growl at 對…咆哮

5. 從未經歷過健康情感關係的人傾向視關係裡的有害特質為理所當然。
   ★ take sth for granted 視…為理所當然

III. Guided Translation

1. ripped; off
2. given; consent
3. rugged; ground
4. alienated; from
5. revolved; around

Round 6

I. Multiple Choice

1. D	2. A	3. C	4. C	5. A
6. A	7. B	8. A	9. A	10. B
11. B	12. A	13. A	14. D	15. C

1. 不管多少錢都無法誘使我離開這份我所熱衷的工作。
   (A) 零售；(B) 使墮落；(C) 使合法；**(D) 誘使**

2. 大部分的時候，Calum 喜愛獨處，而非參與聚會和社交。
   (A) 獨處的；(B) 未開發的；(C) 慣例的；(D) 古銅色的

3. Fallon 和 Conan 的生意由於糟糕的景氣而失敗了，他們因此負債累累。
   (A) 按摩；(B) 發抖；**(C) 使承擔**；(D) 使變軟

4. 市立中學是受該市的教育局監督。
   (A) 凡人的；(B) 郊區的；**(C) 市立的**；(D) 市民的

5. Susie 不想要承擔這個任務，因為她對其中的責任感到懼怕。
   (A) 承擔；(B) 擠滿；(C) 渴望；(D) 浸泡

6. 輪胎因為橡膠與路面的摩擦而磨損。
   (A) 摩擦；(B) 車隊；(C) 骨折；(D) 流質

7. 任何對申請這份工作有興趣的人應於六月底前寄送履歷至人資部門。
   (A) 半徑；**(B) 履歷**；(C) 提醒；(D) 領域

8. 在找伴侶的時候，有些人會更加注意對方是否在智識上與自己相合。
   (A) 相合的；(B) 龐大的；(C) 金髮的；(D) 酒精的

9. 黃石國家公園是我們美國之旅中最精彩的部分。那裡的景致實在壯麗！
   (A) 最精彩之處；(B) 語調；(C) 到期；(D) 競爭

10. 這本小說與它的電影版本有很大的差異。不過，小說和電影皆被認為是成功的。
    (A) 範圍；**(B) 版本**；(C) 卷軸；(D) 刺激

11. 人類應該只將核能利用在對社會有益的事物上。
    (A) 燒烤；**(B) 利用**；(C) 使恢復活力；(D) 鄙視

12. 由於缺乏任何天敵，這個外來種很快地便棲居於這座島上。
    (A) 居住於；(B) 割草；(C) 收割；(D) 緩和

13. 世界各地的佛教徒聚集於此來膜拜這座神聖的佛像。
    (A) 神聖的；(B) 正統的；(C) 忌妒的；(D) 愛國的

14. 科學家最早於三零年代構想出原子彈的概念。十年之後，這個概念就被付諸實行。
    (A) 變得模糊；(B) 拘留；(C) 留下傷疤；**(D) 想出**

15. 隨著病毒不再那麼具威脅性，衛生當局將在大眾運輸配戴口罩的規定改為由個人自行選擇。
    (A) 算術的；(B) 複合的；**(C) 可選擇的**；(D) 省的

II. Fill in the Blank

1. poking	2. hedge	3. rubbish
4. chair	5. plowed	

1. 祕書已在書架間翻找了半個小時，試圖找到一份重要文件。★ poke around 翻找，搜索

2. 許多國家維持強健的軍隊以作為面對任何可能攻擊的防範措施。★ hedge against 防範措施

3. 不要講廢話！你說的完全是錯的！
   ★ rubbish 廢話

4. 我們不知道誰會主持明天的會議，因為我們的主管前幾天突然辭職了。★ chair 主席

5. Donna 的車在閃避迎面而來的卡車時撞上了一棵樹。★ plow into sb/sth (車子等) 撞上…

III. Guided Translation

1. clung; to
2. qualify; for
3. hostile; to
4. made; plea
5. penetrated; through

Round 7

I. Multiple Choice

1. D	2. C	3. D	4. B	5. B
6. B	7. D	8. C	9. C	10. A
11. B	12. B	13. C	14. A	15. D

1. 水痘是具高度傳染力的疾病，因此如果你得到了，你得待在家自我隔離。
   (A) 賺錢的；(B) 遷徙的；(C) 迷人的；**(D) 傳染性的**

2. 為什麼擺著一張憂愁的臉？發生什麼事了嗎？你想要的話可以跟我說。
   (A) 牙科的；(B) 先前的；**(C) 憂愁的**；(D) 馬虎的

3. 人們過去曾認為月球的表面是光滑的；他們不知道它其實充滿坑洞。
   (A) 虧蝕；(B) 球體；(C) 鼻孔；**(D) 坑洞**

4. 我們對那些充滿想像力的藝術家創新的作品感到印象深刻。
   (A) 含蓄的；**(B) 創新的**；(C) 禮貌的；(D) 基本的

5. 隨著新興人工智慧語言模型的問世，有些人認為人工智慧統治人類的預言距實現已經不遠了。
   (A) 營養；**(B) 預言**；(C) 分子；(D) 朝聖者

6. 月考將至，我認為我得待在家裡整個週末來準備。
   (A) 宣稱；**(B) 認為**；(C) 使聽不見；(D) 招致

7. 這位喜劇演員的笑聲很有傳染力，觀眾全都跟著笑了。
   (A) 幻覺的；(B) 內部的；(C) 圓嘟嘟的；**(D) 易感染的**

8. 一名警察被發現與地方幫派勾結，協助非法物質的進口與分銷。
   (A) 遺產；(B) 衛生；**(C) 聯盟 (勾結)**；(D) 階層

9. 在飛機撞進世貿中心之前，許多人看到它掠過紐約的天際線。
   (A) 瀏覽；(B) 繞過；**(C) 掠過**；(D) 評估

10. 新生兒需要接受各種疫苗注射來防治疫病和感染。
    (A) 注射；(B) 含意；(C) 照明；(D) 親密

11. 這份報紙每週會刊登一則地方成功實業家的簡介。
    (A) 里程碑；**(B) 簡介**；(C) 安裝；(D) 比率

12. 在臺灣的外籍老師，不論國籍，都是給付當地貨幣。
    (A) 立法；**(B) 貨幣**；(C) 山；(D) 原子核

13. Kenobi 將軍擅長戰術。這就是為什麼他的士兵能夠在幾個月內就擊敗敵人。
    (A) 復興；(B) 文本；**(C) 戰術**；(D) 磨難

14. Alex 在西洋棋比賽中被機器人打敗而感到丟臉。
    (A) 羞辱；(B) 弓背；(C) 跨越；(D) 騷擾

15. 真空包裝的食物可以保存很久。
    (A) 帆布；(B) 部分；(C) 水泥；**(D) 真空**

II. Fill in the Blank

1. intent	2. converted	3. savage
4. elevate	5. reminiscent	

1. Dawson 非常專注於完成他的研究，完全不想其他事。★ be intent on 執意做…

2. 這艘汰除的蒸汽輪船被改造為一間漂浮餐廳，讓人們能在河上用餐。
   ★ convert sth to 將…轉變為

3. 媒體針對州長的貪腐進行猛烈攻擊，並要求他辭職。★ savage 猛烈的

4. 每當 Owen 感到沮喪時，他就會轉向他最愛的搖滾樂團。他們的音樂總是會提振他的精神。
   ★ elevate 提高

5. 幾部近期的電影在劇情還有在風格上都令人想起七零年代的美國電影。
   ★ be reminiscent of 令人想起…

III. Guided Translation

1. take; precaution
2. with; caution
3. Out; compassion
4. cultural; heritage
5. fell; prey

Round 8

I. Multiple Choice

1. A	2. D	3. B	4. D	5. B
6. B	7. D	8. D	9. C	10. A
11. A	12. D	13. D	14. C	15. D

1. 因為飯店在假期期間通常會客滿，我建議你盡早訂房。
   (A) **建議**；(B) 給予；(C) 玩弄；(D) 復甦

2. 到目前為止，我們尚未找到符合所有必要條件的人來做這份工作。
   (A) 提名；(B) 推薦；(C) 表示；**(D) 條件**

3. 人若對他人懷有怨恨是不可能獲得內心平靜的。
   (A) 樂觀；**(B) 怨恨**；(C) 鼓掌；(D) 專利

4. 這個社區大多數的居民都是年長者。人們喜歡在這裡過退休生活。
   (A) 模式；(B) 劇作家；(C) 避難所；**(D) 居民**

5. 一位優秀的運動員會尊重對手，不論他(她)多麼想在比賽中打敗對方。
   (A) 律師；**(B) 對手**；(C) 女主人；(D) 局外人

6. 作為政府官員，Zack 的誠實和正直贏得了每個人的尊敬。
   (A) 存貨；**(B) 正直**；(C) 整合；(D) 干涉

7. 我一直想學定點跳傘，但問題是我很怕高。
   (A) 解放；(B) 推動；(C) 使著迷；**(D) 使害怕**

8. Jessica 憤慨地責備她的丈夫，因為他不想幫忙照顧小孩。
   (A) 模糊地；(B) 歡樂地；(C) 幸福洋溢地；**(D) 憤慨地**

9. 年長者容易受傷，因為他們的身體逐漸虛弱。
   (A) 有益健康的；(B) 有效的；**(C) 容易…的**；(D) 無價的

10. 現今年輕人的數位知識水準非常高。幾乎每個人都懂如何使用數位裝置。
    (A) 知識；(B) 山崩；(C) 壽命；(D) 負責

11. Vicky 在車禍中受重傷，並馬上被送到外科病房。
    (A) 病房；(B) 走道；(C) 羅盤；(D) 樣本

12. 屬於公眾領域的歌曲可以被任何人使用、重製和發行，而不會產生法律後果。
    (A) 產業；(B) 特許經營權；(C) 住宅；**(D) 領域**

13. 太空船的速度可達每小時兩萬七千公里，使其能脫離地心引力而進入外太空。
    (A) 氣道；(B) 擴音器；(C) 聚光燈；**(D) 太空船**

14. 中國在 1937 年就已和日本處於交戰狀態，比第二次世界大戰爆發還早了兩年。
    (A) 官僚；(B) 仔細檢查；**(C) 戰鬥**；(D) 著迷

15. 整場賽事的總收入，包含轉播權、贊助和門票收入，接近一百萬元。
    (A) 教義；(B) 可能性；(C) 改良；**(D) 贊助**

II. Fill in the Blank

1. scraped	2. ounce	3. shreds
4. presumed	5. smuggling	

1. Ryan 以當單口喜劇演員糊口，靠著勉強夠用的收入過活。★ scrape a living 餬口，勉強度日

2. 如果 White 先生有一點常識的話，他就不會把所有的錢拿去投資股票市場。
   ★ an ounce of common sense 一點點常識

3. 我們辦公室的文件在丟掉之前要先拿去碎掉。
   ★ shred 碎片

4. 人在被定罪之前都是推定無罪的。
   ★ presume 假定

5. 數名軍方人員被抓到大量走私香菸進入國內。
   ★ smuggle sth into 走私…至

III. Guided Translation

1. out; proportion
2. in; torment
3. differentiate; between
4. freaks; out
5. fell; heir

Round 9

I. Multiple Choice

1. D	2. B	3. B	4. A	5. D
6. B	7. A	8. D	9. C	10. A
11. C	12. A	13. B	14. A	15. A

1. Fung 在一場足球比賽中被其中一位敵對球員弄殘，使他再也無法踢球。
   (A) 減輕；(B) 使疲憊；(C) 蹲；**(D) 使跛腳**

2. 在教官的監督下，學生們裝填他們的步槍、瞄準，然後開火。
   (A) 精確；**(B) 監督**；(C) 小包；(D) 名望

3. 這個家庭醜聞嚴重打擊了市長「完美先生」的形象。
   (A) 培養；**(B) 使遭受**；(C) 旋轉；(D) 從…奪去

4. 那場歷史性的演說透過廣播在世界各地轉播。
   (A) 轉播；(B) 暴動；(C) 排練；(D) 繼續

5. 大多數的佛教僧侶會花很多時間冥想，因他們認為這可以幫助他們在宗教信仰上獲得洞見。
   (A) 敘述；(B) 處方簽；(C) 義務；**(D) 冥想**

6. 以前，學生被禁止在學校說方言；否則，他們會面臨懲罰。
   (A) 指令；**(B) 方言**；(C) 區別；(D) 論文

7. 專家才能辨別原稿和複製品。
   (A) 辨別；(B) 消耗；(C) 丟棄；(D) 拆開

8. Jason 獨特的穿搭風格讓他在其他男孩中獨樹一格。
   (A) 迫切的；(B) 集體的；(C) 大面積的；**(D) 獨特的**

9. 政府正努力讓老傳統免於衰微。
   (A) 厄運；(B) 密度；**(C) 衰微**；(D) 代表團

10. Daniel 和 Eva 對兒子的驟逝深感痛苦。
    (A) 使痛苦；(B) 確定；(C) 保護；(D) 暴跌

11. 幾杯紅酒之後，我感到一陣頭暈目眩。
    (A) 奇觀；(B) 交響樂；**(C) 知覺**；(D) 補充物

12. 對情緒的持久壓抑會造成心理健康問題。我們應該在感到有需要時去表達情緒。
    (A) 壓抑；(B) 剝削；(C) 交叉口；(D) 通信

13. 輿論傾向和平。多數人不支持戰爭。但他們必要時會保衛自己。
    (A) 把…塞入；**(B) 傾向**；(C) 使分心；(D) 奉獻

14. 動物化石曾經是骨頭，但在幾百萬年的自然作用下已變成了石頭。
    (A) 骨頭；(B) 分數；(C) 瑣事；(D) 裸體畫

15. Sophia 專攻電腦科學，她在一家提供軟體設計服務的科技公司上班。
    (A) 專攻；(B) 使安心；(C) 獲得；(D) 揮砍

II. Fill in the Blank

1. accommodate	2. resorted	3. evolved
4. sly	5. opt	

1. 有些人覺得適應新工作很困難；他們通常得花一些時間才能夠習慣新環境。
   ★ accommodate (oneself) to 適應…

2. 一群好戰的反叛者訴諸恐怖主義行動來傳達他們的反政府立場。★ resort to 訴諸於…

3. 基因證據顯示人類由猿類演化而來。
   ★ evolve from 由…進化

4. Leo 已經偷偷地跟他的祕書交往五年。這段不倫戀終於在上週曝光。★ on the sly 偷偷地

5. 面臨壓力時，很多男性會選擇吞下，因為他們覺得尋求幫助是懦弱的表現。
   ★ opt to V 選擇做某事

III. Guided Translation

1. in; quest
2. affection; for
3. discreet; inquiries
4. evacuated; from
5. pondered; over

Round 10

I. Multiple Choice

1. A	2. B	3. D	4. B	5. D
6. D	7. C	8. B	9. D	10. A
11. A	12. D	13. D	14. B	15. D

1. 正直的領導者絕不會濫用自己的權力來滿足個人慾望。
   (A) **濫用**；(B) 彈跳；(C) 舉行；(D) 激勵

2. 在美國的某些州，人們在公共場所公開配戴槍械是可容許的。
   (A) 金融的；(B) **可容許的**；(C) 有規律的；(D) 唐突的

3. 乾旱期間，全國各地水庫的水位急遽下降。
   (A) 半島；(B) 棲息地；(C) 大教堂；(D) **蓄水池**

4. 這座城市的街頭小販以騷擾觀光客和販賣假貨而惡名昭彰。
   (A) 多變的；(B) **惡名昭彰的**；(C) 正直的；(D) 合理的

5. 有些政治人物不該被信任，因為他們經常欺騙大眾，以華美言詞遮蔽事實。
   (A) 加強；(B) 在…之前；(C) 對齊；(D) **遮蔽**

6. 當 Mindy 的兒子退伍回家時，她深情地擁抱他。
   (A) 蔑視；(B) 反抗；(C) 使鋒利；(D) **擁抱**

7. 百科全書是一種書或套書，收錄涵蓋各種主題、資訊豐富的文章。
   (A) 幾何學；(B) 索引；(C) **百科全書**；(D) 書法

8. 儘管盡了最大努力，Larry 仍無法對抗水流，而被河水沖走了。
   (A) 永恆；(B) **努力**；(C) 註冊；(D) 倫理

9. 首相詳述他覺得為何再蓋一座核電廠是沒有必要的。
   (A) 護送；(B) 豎起；(C) 等同視之；(D) **詳述**

10. 副總統 Keller 因其推翻總統的企圖被發現而受到流放。
    (A) **流放**；(B) 超越；(C) 突然大叫；(D) 擅長

11. 十二個月大的嬰兒必須要施打麻疹疫苗。
    (A) **疫苗**；(B) 氣喘；(C) 小睡；(D) 獎金

12. 病毒能透過許多方式散布，所以記得要在你的電腦裡安裝防毒軟體。
    (A) 可觀的；(B) 組成的；(C) 活的；(D) **廣泛的**

13. Elena 遭逢了一連串逆境的打擊。她的父親車禍受傷，她的母親被診斷罹患癌症，而她的兒子失業了。
    (A) 電器；(B) 延伸；(C) 子句；(D) **逆轉**

14. 在我來看，摩托車騎士非常脆弱。對他們多數人來說，安全帽是唯一能夠保護他們的東西。
    (A) 進步的；(B) **脆弱的**；(C) 當代的；(D) 膚淺的

15. Christopher 騎馬跌落時摔斷了他的脊椎。這場意外造成他腰部以下癱瘓。
    (A) 場地；(B) 錨；(C) 小河；(D) **脊椎**

II. Fill in the Blank

1. stank	2. obscurity	3. mentality
4. facilitated	5. alliance	

1. Mick 的呼吸散發著大蒜與啤酒的臭味。我沒辦法忍受這個味道！★ stink of 發出…惡臭

2. Marge 一生默默奉獻偏鄉教育，直到一篇新聞報導讓她一夕成名。★ in obscurity 默默地

3. Frank 因懷有快速致富的心態而投入賭博，很快地他便身無分文。★ mentality 心態

4. 臺美之間的政治與經濟合作促進了赴美留學的風潮。★ facilitate 促使

5. 當老師選擇與校方一同反對學生時，學生們感覺受到了背叛。
   ★ in alliance with 與…同聯盟

III. Guided Translation

1. in; manuscript
2. Fortified; with
3. wary; of
4. in; accordance
5. with; awe

Round 11

I. Multiple Choice

1. C	2. A	3. A	4. D	5. C
6. A	7. C	8. B	9. C	10. B
11. B	12. A	13. A	14. C	15. C

1. 這款空氣清淨機的其中一項特色是能幫助過濾掉空氣中的灰塵。
   (A) 躊躇；(B) 修剪；**(C) 過濾**；(D) 快速移動

2. 僱主經常會提供獎金作為誘因，讓員工更努力工作，為公司創造更多利潤。
   (A) 誘因；(B) 青春痘；(C) 捐款；(D) 一份

3. 軍人必須毫不猶豫執行長官的命令。
   (A) 執行；(B) 改變；(C) 增加；(D) 維持

4. 我們坐在一棵大樹下，它的葉子與樹枝交疊，完全遮住太陽。
   (A) 淨化；(B) 培養；(C) 使成為三倍；**(D) 重疊**

5. Phil 的醫生讓他接受兩週的抗生素療程以治療他的感染。
   (A) 新事物；(B) 營養素；**(C) 抗生素**；(D) 症狀

6. 富人在派對上穿著奢華的服裝來展示他們的財富與地位。
   (A) 服裝；(B) 執行令；(C) 象徵；(D) 床墊

7. 臺灣黑熊是瀕危的物種。如果人們不想辦法保護牠們，牠們可能會絕種。
   (A) 過度的；(B) 外部的；**(C) 滅絕的**；(D) 行政的

8. 學生被鼓勵去參與課外活動，因這被認為能夠幫助他們人格發展。
   (A) 憲法允許的；**(B) 課外的**；(C) 住宅的；(D) 外向的

9. Alex 從未結婚，因為他認為在這個瞬息萬變的世界中不可能找到永恆的愛。
   (A) 可想像的；(B) 暫定的；**(C) 永恆的**；(D) 謹慎小心的

10. 衛生官員警告大眾，表示今年冬天將會爆發流感疫情。
    (A) 前景；**(B) 爆發**；(C) 出遊；(D) 憤怒

11. 先祖的精神仍淌流於我的血管中。我和昔日的他們一樣渴望去探索世界。
    (A) 垂直面；**(B) 血管**；(C) 小販；(D) 人聲演唱

12. 即使已在西方國家居住多年，這些難民仍經常感到旁人的敵意。
    (A) 敵意；(B) 征服；(C) 移植；(D) 獲得

13. Nelson 在那場街頭鬥毆中心臟中刀，當場死亡。
    (A) 當場地；(B) 因此；(C) 片刻；(D) 在空中

14. Nora 在與她最好的朋友吵架之後，就發誓再也不跟她說話。
    (A) 暴增；(B) 哀悼；**(C) 發誓**；(D) 出價

15. Karl 是個可悲的人。即便他想要受人喜愛，且急於討好身邊的人，他還是沒有真正的朋友。
    (A) 粗俗的；(B) 多愁善感的；**(C) 悲慘的**；(D) 字面的

II. Fill in the Blank

1. mortgage	2. obliged	3. surge
4. grilled	5. hacking	

1. Roland 花了二十年的辛苦歲月才還清他的房貸。★ pay off a mortgage 清償房貸

2. 由於在派對上玩得非常盡興，我覺得我得要給男女主辦人一張感謝的字條。
   ★ feel obliged to 感到有義務去…

3. 當 Arvin 看到一個帥氣的男生正陪同他喜歡的男孩時，他內心充滿一陣忌妒。
   ★ a surge of 一陣

4. Gary 連續兩天被警察審問關於他同夥藏身處的資訊，但他仍拒絕鬆口。★ grill 長時間審問

5. Luther 因駭進好幾家銀行的電腦系統並竊走大量金錢而被通緝。★ hack into 駭入

III. Guided Translation

1. immune; to
2. in; procession
3. under; illusion
4. in; anticipation
5. On; assumption

Round 12

I. Multiple Choice

1. C	2. A	3. B	4. A	5. C
6. B	7. C	8. A	9. D	10. B
11. C	12. A	13. B	14. A	15. C

1. 如果你想要你花園裡的植物茁壯，你得要把土壤變得肥沃。
   (A) 枯萎；(B) 死亡；**(C) 茁壯**；(D) 顫抖

2. Preston 在機場忙亂地找尋他的護照，而距他的飛機起飛只剩一小時。
   (A) 忙亂地；(B) 強健地；(C) 鬼鬼祟祟地；(D) 策略上地

3. 在加護病房內，虛弱的病人受到全天候照顧。
   (A) 惡意的；**(B) 虛弱的**；(C) 一致同意的；(D) 魯莽的

4. 藥劑師應該複查醫師的處方箋以避免出錯。
   (A) 藥劑師；(B) 傳教士；(C) 檢察官；(D) 裁判

5. 醫師警告不良姿勢會導致嚴重的脊椎問題。
   (A) 經濟蕭條；(B) 遷徙；**(C) 姿勢**；(D) 開端

6. 警察要目擊者不要再給他瑣碎的細節，只管回答問的問題就好。
   (A) 強效的；**(B) 瑣碎的**；(C) 首要的；(D) 通靈的

7. 我們在古董店購買這個花瓶的時候沒有注意到它的瑕疵，現在要退貨已經太遲了。
   (A) 敵人；(B) 家禽；**(C) 瑕疵**；(D) 犯規

8. 每一位超過七十歲的年長者會獲得一份新臺幣三千元的老年退休金。
   (A) 退休金；(B) 原型；(C) 諺語；(D) 農民

9. 這座城鎮的人正在抵制這家店，因為它販賣過期商品。
   (A) 主張；(B) 提升；(C) 記錄；**(D) 抵制**

10. 我們的盟友沒有遺棄我們，現在正前來幫助我們。我們將能抵擋邪惡，最終邁向勝利。
    (A) 傳教；**(B) 遺棄**；(C) 侵擾；(D) 激怒

11. 這裡所有的房間都是套房，因此不需要跟其他人共用廁所和廚房。
    (A) 行人；(B) 閣樓；**(C) 套房**；(D) 貧民窟

12. 漫威工作室和數家品牌聯名合作，發行一系列官方商品。
    (A) 商品；(B) 共產主義；(C) 獨創性；(D) 模稜兩可

13. 你的作文清晰明瞭，且很有組織，但你還是應該避免錯字之類的小錯誤。
    (A) 叛逆的；**(B) 微不足道的**；(C) 瘋狂的；(D) 未受損的

14. 如果你希望升等到頭等艙，你需要再支付額外費用。
    (A) 升級；(B) 用帶子繫；(C) 更新；(D) 纏結

15. 阿波羅 11 號，作為首次將人類送至月球表面的太空任務，在萬眾光芒下展開。
    (A) 啜泣；(B) 後院；**(C) 火焰**；(D) 棺材

II. Fill in the Blank

1. inevitable	2. projection	3. captives
4. bosom	5. blunt	

1. 你必須要接受無可避免的事實，準備隨時和你的母親告別。★ the inevitable 無可避免之事

2. Kennedy 被主管指派去做下一季的利潤預測。
   ★ projection 預測

3. 成千上萬的盟軍俘虜在德國人無條件投降後從戰俘營中獲釋。★ captive 俘虜

4. 這些難民一抵達他們的新家，就受到當地社群由衷的歡迎。
   ★ in the bosom of sth 在…的關懷裡

5. 你或許覺得不中聽，但坦白說，你最近表現得不是很好。★ to be blunt 坦白說，直話直說

III. Guided Translation

1. full; vitality
2. on; brink
3. reached; accommodation
4. infer; from
5. conform; to

Round 13

I. Multiple Choice

1. B	2. C	3. C	4. B	5. C
6. C	7. D	8. C	9. C	10. A
11. C	12. B	13. A	14. D	15. D

1. 警察在將嫌犯羈押前做了一些初步的調查。
   (A) 負有責任的；(B) **初步的**；(C) 依賴的；(D) 可行的

2. Saoirse 在樹林裡散步時絆到了木頭而跌倒在地。
   (A) 滑行；(B) 與…對峙；(C) **絆到**；(D) 使變成

3. 總統女士對世界和平的貢獻為她的國家帶來卓著的聲望。
   (A) 儲存；(B) 官僚體系；(C) **聲望**；(D) 能力

4. Rena 因不良行為而受到停學處分。
   (A) 繼承；(B) **停學**；(C) 擴大；(D) 處理

5. 美國數州通過了禁止在公共場所吸菸的法律。
   (A) 動員；(B) 使和解；(C) **禁止**；(D) 橫跨

6. Fabre 在追逐花園裡的蝴蝶後氣喘吁吁。
   (A) 閃爍；(B) 悲痛；(C) **喘氣**；(D) 產生

7. 在夢裡，我們同為夢中世界的建築師和探索者，因為我們同時建構與經歷夢境。
   (A) 捐贈者；(B) 名人；(C) 子女；(D) **建築師**

8. 這位新娘穿的婚紗真是漂亮極了。她看起來魅力四射！
   (A) 榮譽的；(B) 可笑的；(C) **非常漂亮的**；(D) 虛擬的

9. 變成熟是一個累積的過程。你不能期待自己只是因為到了某個年紀就突然搞懂所有事情。
   (A) 奇蹟似的；(B) 休閒娛樂的；(C) **累積的**；(D) 運作的

10. 大使館拒絕發給我入境簽證；因此，我無法跟我的家人團圓。
    (A) **給予**；(B) 接近；(C) 妥協；(D) 推測

11. 你或許完全了解書上的理論，但它無法代替實際經驗。
    (A) 傷感；(B) 賠償金；(C) **替代品**；(D) 無聊

12. Sandra 具有關於二十世紀臺灣文學的深刻知識。
    (A) 批發的；(B) **深奧的**；(C) 言語的；(D) 輻射的

13. 房東要他的租客離開，因為他們已經三個月沒繳房租了。
    (A) **租客**；(B) 戰利品；(C) 受託人；(D) 大腿

14. 我覺得我因為我的性別和公民身分而受到歧視了。
    (A) 壯麗；(B) 實體；(C) 人員；(D) **公民身分**

15. 昨晚土石流掩埋了整個村莊而造成滅村，真的是場大災難。
    (A) 誇大；(B) 驚悚片；(C) 死傷者；(D) **大災難**

II. Fill in the Blank

1. phased	2. pipeline	3. slot
4. toll	5. irritated	

1. 新貨幣正以分段的方式取代舊貨幣。
   ★ phase in 分段實施

2. 我們的新電腦系統正在規劃當中，下週就可以準備好運作。★ in the pipeline 正在進行中

3. 你可以幫我把其中一張德布西的唱片放入 CD 播放器嗎？★ slot into 將…插入或投入溝槽中

4. 新冠疫情的封城對學生的學業表現和人際互動能力造成損害。
   ★ take a toll (on sb/sth) (對…) 造成損害

5. 陳老師被她學生搗蛋的行為惹惱，決定罰他們留校察看。★ irritate 使惱怒

III. Guided Translation

1. biased; against
2. in; chaos
3. precedence; over
4. insights; into
5. climaxed; with

Round 14

I. Multiple Choice

1. B	2. B	3. C	4. A	5. C
6. D	7. A	8. A	9. B	10. D
11. D	12. B	13. A	14. A	15. B

1. 在選務人員計算完選票之前，選舉的結果不會確定。
   (A) 栗子；(B) **選票**；(C) 陪審團；(D) 請願書

2. 有關當局告誡民眾，由於颱風將至，不要造訪濱海景點。
   (A) 將…鍍鎳；(B) **告誡**；(C) 調解；(D) 閒逛

3. Dominick 的總年收入破百萬，這就是為什麼他能夠負擔得起市區的房子。
   (A) 男同性戀的；(B) 地理的；(C) **總共的**；(D) 陰暗的

4. 什麼都無法彌補你浪費掉的時間；從現在起你最好別再瞎混了。
   (A) **彌補**；(B) 實施；(C) 抑制；(D) 包辦宴席

5. 為了要強化軍力，政府將招募更多軍人。
   (A) 批准；(B) 環繞；(C) **招募**；(D) 朗誦

6. 暴政其實是懼怕人民的；它們只是將之隱藏在各種殘酷和獨裁的舉措之下。
   (A) 克制；(B) 租金；(C) 爬蟲類；(D) **政權**

7. 看！道路兩側都有牛群在吃草。
   (A) **吃草**；(B) 吞食；(C) 捕食；(D) 燉煮

8. 聖火傳遞是運動會中的一項儀式。當火炬點燃後，它將會在全國傳遞。
   (A) **火炬**；(B) 折磨；(C) 龍捲風；(D) 急流

9. 隨著人類製造的溫室氣體增加，全球暖化也跟著加劇，因為這些氣體會吸收太陽輻射。
   (A) 領悟；(B) **輻射**；(C) 揭露；(D) 修復

10. 灌木圍繞著原野上的那棟木屋，使其隱蔽於視線之外。
    (A) 怒視；(B) 租約；(C) 一批；(D) **灌木**

11. 希斯‧萊傑扮演的小丑被普遍認為是史上最經典的電影惡棍之一。
    (A) 否決權；(B) 抵用券；(C) (有風險的) 企業；(D) **惡棍**

12. 政府官員考慮推動稅務體系的全面改革，以期望增加稅收。
    (A) 啟發；(B) **考慮**；(C) 暗殺；(D) 欺騙

13. 慘澹的經濟前景及惡化的環境條件對年輕世代造成不利的情勢。
    (A) **不利的**；(B) 職業的；(C) 有手腕的；(D) 有條理的

14. 如果你這麼痛恨你的工作，就離職去找更好的。整天坐在這抱怨連連是沒有用的。
    (A) **呻吟**；(B) 臉紅；(C) 迷路；(D) 閃爍

15. 令大家感到驚訝的是，這支業餘隊伍在冰上曲棍錦標賽打敗了職業隊伍。
    (A) 議會；(B) **錦標賽**；(C) 交替；(D) 大公司

II. Fill in the Blank

1. presumption	2. intervals	3. slammed
4. deter	5. sequence	

1. 這所學校所有的規定都是以人性本善為假定去制訂的。
   ★ on the presumption that 以…為假定

2. 捷運列車每天早上六點到凌晨十二點以規律的間距從終點站發車。
   ★ at regular intervals 相隔一定的時間或距離

3. 當 Simon 向 Olivia 尋求協助時，他被悍然拒絕。★ slam the door in sb's face 悍然拒絕…

4. 我們希望這個新的政治聯盟能夠阻止某些國家做出任何可能破壞區域和平的魯莽行為。
   ★ deter sb from (doing) sth 阻止某人做某事

5. 這個系統只能依照特定程序啟動，否則它會自己上鎖。★ in a . . . sequence 以…的順序

III. Guided Translation

1. with; certainty
2. life; span
3. at; random
4. bomb; squad
5. commentary; on

Round 15

I. Multiple Choice

1. A	2. D	3. A	4. A	5. D
6. A	7. D	8. C	9. B	10. C
11. A	12. B	13. B	14. D	15. C

1. Sally 的新書是對她已故外公的致敬，他是一名沙場老兵。
   (A) **表尊敬**；(B) 衡量標準；(C) 變動；(D) 受訪者

2. 長時間的乾旱導致了該國的用水與食物短缺，其人民急需國際援助。
   (A) 石油；(B) 持續時間；(C) 開銷；(D) **乾旱**

3. Dalton 是美國西部知名的不法之徒之一，他槍殺了許多的對手。
   (A) **不法之徒**；(B) 群；(C) 宴會；(D) 收受者

4. Spencer 夫人很年輕就成為寡婦了。 她的丈夫很久之前就去世了。
   (A) **寡婦**；(B) 學徒；(C) 複製品；(D) 香味

5. 別輕易相信你在網路上讀到的所有東西。上面的資訊並非都是可信的。
   (A) 乏味的；(B) 包含的；(C) 微妙的；(D) **可信的**

6. Penny 長年被大洪水沖走她家園的記憶糾纏。
   (A) **使困擾**；(B) 歡呼；(C) 阻礙；(D) 利用

7. 前首相的阿茲海默症在他開始失去時間感時變得明顯。
   (A) 至高無上的；(B) 比較的；(C) 結構上的；(D) **明顯的**

8. 八名美國人在西亞旅行時被一群恐怖分子挾持為人質。
   (A) 贊助者；(B) 家禽；(C) **人質**；(D) 拘留

9. Cena 總統屈服於民意，並啟動憲法改革。
   (A) 濃縮；(B) **屈服**；(C) 徒步旅行；(D) 反駁

10. William 對他年邁的父母漠不關心，他很少陪伴他們。
    (A) 極大的；(B) 帝國的；(C) **漠不關心的**；(D) 無限的

11. 不同文化的問候儀式有所不同，所以我們必須意識到其差異。
    (A) **儀式**；(B) 差事；(C) 競技場；(D) 設施

12. 一隻老鷹在原野上盤旋，搜索兔子和其他小動物。
    (A) 亂塞；(B) **盤旋**；(C) 嗶嗶叫；(D) 拖著腳走

13. Morty 的狗在門口哀鳴，要求被放出房外。
    (A) 聳肩；(B) **哀鳴**；(C) 逐漸損害；(D) 使人想起

14. 宗教給人勇氣並教導人即便在最黑暗的時刻都不要絕望。
    (A) 融化；(B) 衰退；(C) 使顯得矮小；(D) **絕望**

15. 婚禮中，新郎掀起新娘的面紗並親吻了她。
    (A) 少女；(B) 雜務；(C) **面紗**；(D) 假髮

II. Fill in the Blank

1. consultation	2. warded	3. core
4. swamped	5. swap	

1. Wendy 與父母和老師諮詢後決定了她的大學主修。★ in consultation with sb 與某人諮詢

2. 這名拳擊手敏捷地閃過對手的出擊，並予以反擊。★ ward off 避開

3. 當我聽到一個我極為敬重的人說出如此惡毒的話時，我感到徹底的震驚。
   ★ to the core 徹底的

4. Patrick 整個暑假都在玩耍，如今他被沒寫完的作業給淹沒了。
   ★ be swamped with sth 被某事淹沒

5. Marianne 要 Connell 跟她換位子，這樣她才能跟坐他旁邊的帥哥講話。★ swap 交換

III. Guided Translation

1. made; commitment
2. in; astonishment
3. in; abundance
4. subordinate; to
5. subscribe; to

Round 16

I. Multiple Choice

1. C	2. D	3. B	4. B	5. B
6. C	7. B	8. D	9. A	10. A
11. B	12. B	13. A	14. D	15. B

1. 暖氣機在如此冷冽的冬天裡是不可或缺的。
   (A) 可相比的；(B) 貧瘠的；(C) **不可或缺的**；(D) 沙啞的

2. 沿途公路的單調景致讓我們南向的旅途十分無聊。
   (A) 清楚；(B) 流利；(C) 總統任期；(D) **單調**

3. Jackson 良好的行為舉止反映了他兒時有紀律的教育。
   (A) 連續的；(B) **反映出⋯的**；(C) 敘述的；(D) 立法的

4. Moss 爬到樹上以取回卡在樹枝上的風箏。
   (A) 堅持；(B) **取回**；(C) 壓扁；(D) 騎腳踏車

5. 我要坦白一件事：昨晚是我把你的海綿蛋糕全吃掉的。
   (A) 機件；(B) **坦白**；(C) 過敏；(D) 虧損

6. 反對黨成員譴責這場展覽會是執政黨的政治宣傳。
   (A) 起訴；(B) 主權；(C) **政治宣傳**；(D) 計算

7. 管理階層對工會做出讓步，並同意實施加薪。
   (A) 攝取；(B) **讓步**；(C) 屍體；(D) 兆

8. 少年犯罪日益嚴重，促使市政府調查為何青少年會被驅使去犯罪。
   (A) 軍事的；(B) 司法的；(C) 中立的；(D) **少年的**

9. Ridley 的傲慢使得每個人都離他而去。人們真的無法忍受他的自負。
   (A) **傲慢**；(B) 詮釋；(C) 機構；(D) 墮胎

10. 為何 Lesley 說她要出城，但卻在車站留連呢？
    (A) **留連**；(B) 傳播；(C) 培養；(D) 乘船遊覽

11. 近期研究已經確立過長的螢幕使用時間與心理疲勞的相關性。
    (A) 訴訟；(B) **相關性**；(C) 方程式；(D) 轉變

12. Lowe 覺得他襯衫的硬領簡直要勒死他了。他幾乎不能呼吸。
    (A) 舒緩；(B) **勒死**；(C) 弄髒；(D) 弄碎

13. 這家奢華五星級飯店的大廳舖飾著一張覆蓋整個地面的豪華地毯。
    (A) **豪華的**；(B) 清澈的；(C) 後面的；(D) 外國的

14. 在《魔戒》裡，即便是能力強大的巫師都不敢拿取至尊戒，以免被邪惡力量誘惑。
    (A) 同樣地；(B) 因此；(C) 然而；(D) **以免**

15. Cobain 在吉他上刷了幾個和弦，以確認吉他是否已經調好音。
    (A) 海峽；(B) **和弦**；(C) 母音；(D) 審計

II. Fill in the Blank

1. aspired	2. incorporate	3. perspective
4. tuition	5. siege	

1. 自小，Katherine 就渴望太空探索的志業。
   ★ aspire 渴望

2. Tim 試圖將地方元素融入新市政府大樓的設計中。★ incorporate sth into sth 將⋯包含至⋯

3. 理性看事情的話，當前我們除了手邊有的這個辦法之外，並沒有其他替代方案。
   ★ put sth in/into perspective 理性看待某事

4. 美國的大學學費是眾所皆知地昂貴，所以很多學生別無選擇只能申請學生貸款。
   ★ tuition 學費

5. 媒體包圍了飯店，等待巨星現身。
   ★ lay siege to 包圍⋯

III. Guided Translation

1. departure; lounge
2. impulse; to
3. subsequent; to
4. descend; from
5. removal; of

Round 17

I. Multiple Choice

1. D	2. A	3. A	4. C	5. D
6. B	7. A	8. B	9. C	10. B
11. A	12. A	13. D	14. B	15. A

1. 一些學生因嘲弄剛從國外回來的新同學的口音而被老師責罵。
   (A) 證實；(B) 屠殺；(C) 無意間聽到；(D) **嘲弄**

2. 顧客選擇我們是因為我們提供的周到服務在同業中無人能及。
   (A) **周到的**；(B) 詩的；(C) 過敏的；(D) 被免除的

3. 科學家表示這個公共衛生問題的規模超乎想像。
   (A) **規模**；(B) 尿布；(C) 直徑；(D) 通訊錄

4. Angie 有被前男友劈腿的糟糕經驗；因此，她無法忍受他是很正常的。
   (A) 摘錄；(B) 判斷；(C) **忍受**；(D) 摔角

5. 在三萬英呎的高度，機外溫度大約是攝氏零下四十度。
   (A) 態度；(B) 獨處；(C) 學院；(D) **高度**

6. 該名警官因違反了執法程序而被要求繳出他的徽章和配槍。
   (A) 奪取；(B) **徽章**；(C) 碼頭；(D) 睫毛

7. 你的 T 恤上有一塊髒汙。你應該用漂白劑把它洗掉。
   (A) **漂白劑**；(B) 布料；(C) 光芒；(D) 天鵝絨

8. Ashley 的兒子在操場上跌倒擦傷了他的膝蓋。
   (A) 把…塞進；(B) **碰傷**；(C) 使堅硬；(D) 搖擺

9. 在過去，水手依賴星宿和羅盤來導航船隻。
   (A) 現代化；(B) 教化；(C) **導航**；(D) 宣傳

10. 整個村莊受到敵方轟炸機轟炸並摧毀。
    (A) 預想；(B) **爆破**；(C) 結巴；(D) 統一

11. 跟學生解釋規則時必須要明確，否則他們無法理解。
    (A) **明白清楚的**；(B) 道德的；(C) 異國風味的；(D) 外面的

12. 警方的警告僅有微幅的效果。許多人仍被騙去柬埔寨從事非法工作。
    (A) **些微的**；(B) 極地的；(C) 值得的；(D) 空前的

13. 戰爭期間，一名士兵最不該做的就是背叛自己的國家。
    (A) 爆發；(B) 熱愛；(C) 懇求；(D) **背叛**

14. 不要讓你的小孩把小玩具或鈕扣放到口中，以免他們噎到或窒息。
    (A) 打鼾；(B) **窒息**；(C) 激動；(D) 拖拉

15. 運河被開鑿以將沙漠變成富饒之地，讓人們可在其上生產作物。
    (A) **運河**；(B) 國界；(C) 礁石；(D) 探查

II. Fill in the Blank

1. alternated	2. ripple	3. convicted
4. particle	5. agony	

1. 當 Henley 聽到這個壞消息,他時而憤怒時而又陷入絕望。★ alternate 交替

2. 當市長宣布他不會競選連任的時候,會議室裡激起了一陣驚呼。★ a ripple of 一陣

3. Vincent 又被抓到在店裡偷東西了。 他將第二次因商店行竊而被宣判有罪。
   ★ be convicted of 被以…宣判有罪

4. 這名獨裁者被專業殺手暗殺了,現場沒有留下任何一點證據。★ a particle of 極少量的…

5. 車禍的傷者痛苦地躺在路中間,等待救護車到來。★ in agony 極度痛苦

III. Guided Translation

1. sexual; harassment
2. take; oath
3. mingle; with
4. national; anthem
5. launched; assault

Round 18

I. Multiple Choice

1. C	2. D	3. C	4. A	5. B
6. A	7. D	8. D	9. B	10. D
11. B	12. D	13. C	14. C	15. A

1. 我家後院佇立著一棵強壯的老橡樹，我們小時候常會攀爬它。
   (A) 可食的；(B) 懲戒的；(**C**) **強壯的**；(D) 過早的

2. 在新冠疫情的巔峰時期，成千上萬的人被關在家中、飯店房間和醫院病房裡。
   (A) 流出；(B) 堅持；(C) 注射；(**D**) **關住**

3. Manson 嬉皮的外貌已變成他的特徵。 他留著長髮且總是穿著喇叭牛仔褲。
   (A) 腫塊；(B) 恥辱；(**C**) **特徵**；(D) 航空

4. Mandy 穿著那件深綠色的絲絨連身裙好看極了。她今晚一定會成為全場焦點。
   (**A**) **很棒的**；(B) 芳香的；(C) 有限的；(D) 即將到來的

5. 這位老婦人對任何拜訪她的人都很友好。她會以茶和餅乾歡迎他們。
   (A) 迷人的；(**B**) **友好的**；(C) 生動的；(D) 有毒的

6. Katie 將一個大型娃娃緊抱於懷中， 這是她父親送她的生日禮物。
   (**A**) **抱緊**；(B) 使豐富；(C) 沉迷；(D) 滴答響

7. Collins 一家搬到在郊區的新房子，與市中心之間具有便利的通勤距離。
   (A) 使反轉；(B) 使吃驚；(C) 移植；(**D**) **通勤**

8. 這把口袋刀是一種多功能的工具，可以作為螺絲起子、鑽子、開瓶器和剪刀。
   (A) 激進的；(B) 有能力的；(C) 同時的；(**D**) **多功能的**

9. 新法的反對者譴責它為對於人身自由的攻擊。
   (A) 修正；(**B**) **譴責**；(C) 查詢；(D) 吃驚

10. 這棟建築物展現完美的對稱，其兩邊的形狀吻合。
    (A) 醜聞；(B) 垂直面；(C) 刻板印象；(**D**) **對稱**

11. 一群員警在事故發生的現場進行監督。
    (A) 包含；(**B**) **監督**；(C) 開藥；(D) 抵觸

12. 人們一直渴望著一個愛、和平與平等盛行的烏托邦，但往往事與願違。
    (A) 召集；(B) 作證；(C) 隱瞞；(**D**) **盛行**

13. 山坡上的石牆是一座十四世紀古城堡的遺跡。
    (A) 汙漬；(B) 綠洲；(**C**) **遺跡**；(D) 神話

14. 你知道誰會擔任我們國家參與今年 APEC 的代表嗎？
    (A) 合併；(B) 愛國者；(**C**) **代表**；(D) 叛徒

15. 雖然使用清潔劑洗碗很方便，但重要的是需留意很多清潔劑對環境有害。
    (**A**) **清潔劑**；(B) 賽馬騎師；(C) 中士；(D) 橫布條

II. Fill in the Blank

1. merges	2. synthetic	3. vomit
4. indigenous	5. brace	

1. 蜂鳴與鳥啼融合而成了一部美麗的自然交響曲。★ merge with 與…融合

2. 這件洋裝由合成纖維製成，好讓它能夠丟洗衣機洗。★ synthetic 合成的

3. 令人作嘔的味道使得 Derek 吐出了他吃下的東西。★ vomit up 嘔吐

4. 毛利語是紐西蘭原住民所使用的本土語言。
   ★ indigenous 本土的

5. 當飛機準備在水面緊急降落時，空服員指示所有乘客做好應對衝擊的準備。
   ★ brace 使做好準備

III. Guided Translation

1. analogy; between
2. monopoly; on
3. Hormone; balance
4. abbreviation; for
5. contempt; for

Round 19

I. Multiple Choice

1. C	2. D	3. C	4. D	5. C
6. C	7. C	8. B	9. B	10. B
11. C	12. D	13. A	14. C	15. A

1. 搭乘電扶梯的時候，人們通常會站在右側，以
讓趕時間的人用左側通行。
   (A) 作品集；(B) 體裁；(**C**) **電扶梯**；(D) 寓言

2. 敵軍人數可能多於我軍，但我們的士氣比他們
高昂。
   (A) 說；(B) 拒絕提供；(C) 委任；(**D**) **數量上超過**

3. Kelly 的性格坦率。她對自己有自信，同時也
不害怕承認自己的缺點。
   (A) 複數的；(B) 僵硬的；(**C**) **坦率的**；(D) 即將發
生的

4. 史蒂芬‧金是一位著名的驚悚小說家。他的某
些小說有被改編成電影。
   (A) 中世紀的；(B) 近視的；(C) 模糊不清的；(**D**)
著名的

5. 為了研究極地環境，科學家出發前往南極探
險。
   (A) 抽象；(B) 短缺；(**C**) **遠征**；(D) 種植場

6. 這位知名的羽球選手擊敗了對手，拿下了女子
單打的第四連勝。
   (A) 有望的；(B) 象徵的；(**C**) **連續的**；(D) 本土的

7. 政府所實施的無效經濟政策加速了製造業的
衰微。
   (A) 使沮喪；(B) 粉碎；(**C**) **促進**；(D) 禁止

8. Hughes 的上司召集他開會討論他的表現，而他
依規出席。
   (A) 大概；(**B**) **照著**；(C) 理論上；(D) 惡意地

9. 管理階層應該讓資訊取得更加容易，這樣所有
員工才知道公司有什麼事正在發展。
   (A) 熱中的；(**B**) **容易得到的**；(C) 強制的；(D) 自
發的

10. 為提升這部越戰紀錄片的可信度，劇組邀請幾
位老兵來講述他們的故事。
    (A) 調解；(**B**) **敘述**；(C) 創始；(D) 放射

11. Mitch 對藝術極富熱忱，逐年累積了令人印象
深刻的畫作與古董收藏。
    (A) 使著迷；(B) 安慰；(**C**) **累積**；(D) 使減到最低

12. 蝙蝠具有銳利的聽覺，狗則具有靈敏的嗅覺。
    (A) 古怪的；(B) 直覺的；(C) 有效的；(**D**) **敏銳的**

13. 在你能經營一間公司之前，你需要有大量的管
理經驗。
    (**A**) **管理**；(B) 主權；(C) 生育能力；(D) 團結

14. 政府撥出了新臺幣七百億給創造就業的計畫。
    (A) 照亮；(B) 把…歸因於…；(**C**) **撥出**；(D) 密謀

15. 臺灣因其戰略地理位置而成為東亞的一個經
濟與政治中心。
    (**A**) **戰略的**；(B) 唯一的；(C) 精彩的；(D) 靜止不
動的

II. Fill in the Blank

1. prosecuted	2. pillar	3. denial
4. stake	5. rips/ripped	

1. 幾名警察因為對嫌犯肢體暴力而受到起訴。
   ★ be prosecuted for 被以…起訴

2. 不要對作為社會的中堅分子感到過度自滿，因
為能力越大，責任就越大。
   ★ a pillar of society 社會的中堅分子

3. 即使氣候變遷災難的危險是非常真實的，氣候
變遷否定論仍持續存在於世界上許多地方。
   ★ denial 否認

4. 如果我們繼續對極端天氣的議題視之不理，年
輕世代的未來將處於危險中。
   ★ at stake 處於危險中

5. Edward 看到他的兒子臥床且靠著插管維生，令
他撕心裂肺。★ rip 撕裂

III. Guided Translation

1. make; fuss
2. grumble; about
3. in; rash
4. metaphor; for
5. prone; to

Round 20

I. Multiple Choice

1. A	2. B	3. A	4. B	5. A
6. A	7. B	8. A	9. C	10. A
11. B	12. C	13. B	14. B	15. A

1. 楊紫瓊是一位有名的電影明星；她不僅在香港也在好萊塢的許多武打片中擔任主角。
   (A) **有名的**；(B) 極膽小的；(C) 離譜的；(D) 本質上的

2. 政府正計畫從北方轉移水資源以緩解南方水情吃緊的壓力。
   (A) 精神創傷；(B) **轉移**；(C) 挫折；(D) 前例

3. 當我登機時，一名空服員沿著走道引導我到我的座位。
   (A) **引導**；(B) 召喚；(C) 保護；(D) 拓展

4. Carson 是個偽君子，因為他在公開場合支持性別運動，但在私下卻表達歧視女性的言論。
   (A) 優勝者；(B) **偽君子**；(C) 政治家；(D) 聖人

5. 一個有能力的政府應該努力確保社會中的每一位成員都沒有受到排除。
   (A) **排除**；(B) 嘶叫；(C) 使均等；(D) 劫持

6. 現今，你可以在幾乎每間公共廁所找到分配肥皂和衛生紙的機器。
   (A) **分配**；(B) 震動；(C) 搶救；(D) 閃耀

7. Gibson 命中註定要成為人民的領袖並引領他們獲得自由。
   (A) 生態；(B) **命運**；(C) 穩定；(D) 墓地

8. Andy 因為再也無法忍受他老闆傲慢的態度而辭掉了工作。
   (A) **傲慢的**；(B) 有資格的；(C) 適用的；(D) 有同情心的

9. 自從 Eugene 從那個夏令營回來之後，他的行為就變得很異常。不知道他在那邊發生了什麼事。
   (A) 精心製作的；(B) 認知的；(C) **異常的**；(D) 大都市的

10. 日本對珍珠港蓄意的攻擊促使美國加入第二次世界大戰。
    (A) **刻意的**；(B) 匿名的；(C) 機密的；(D) 有說服力的

11. 在那邊的詢問臺可以取得免費的渡假資訊小冊子。
    (A) 格局；(B) **小冊子**；(C) 公民投票；(D) 投手

12. 這兩國的談判代表在軍備控制的會談上達成歷史性的突破，這真是個好消息。
    (A) 破裂；(B) 鎮壓；(C) **突破**；(D) 崩潰

13. 有些鳥能夠模仿牠們周圍環境的聲音。
    (A) 茂盛；(B) **模仿**；(C) 同情；(D) 使癱瘓

14. 冰河經由雪的堆積而形成，期間雪逐漸被壓縮成巨大的冰體。
    (A) 鳥啼；(B) **冰河**；(C) 顫抖；(D) 龐然大物

15. 照片下方的說明文字寫著：「至今每年仍有數百萬人死於飢餓。」
    (A) **說明文字**；(B) 嘲諷；(C) 座右銘；(D) 配額

II. Fill in the Blank

1. stabilized	2. vapors	3. compelled
4. thefts	5. uprising	

1. 隨著疾病的成因被發現，且越來越多人受到治癒，這場公衛危機終於逐漸穩定。
   ★ stabilize 使穩定

2. 水蒸氣上升至高空並凝結成雲，然後以雨或雪的形式回到地面。★ water vapor 水蒸氣

3. 都市擴張迫使許多野生動物離開牠們的棲息地，並學習在人類文明的陰影下存活。
   ★ compel 迫使

4. 我聽說這個街坊不是很安全。最近已經有好幾起竊盜的通報。★ theft 竊盜

5. 面對人民暴動，這位獨裁者別無選擇只好下臺並流亡海外。★ popular uprising 人民暴動

III. Guided Translation

1. charitable; organizations
2. bears; resemblance
3. no; coincidence
4. destructive; to
5. reliance; on

Review 1

I. Multiple Choice

1. A	2. C	3. C	4. B	5. C
6. B	7. D	8. C	9. D	10. A
11. A	12. B	13. A	14. C	15. B

1. 已經九點四十分了，但 Olive 還是沒有跟我們聯繫。她可能又要遲到了。
   (A) **聯繫**；(B) 鏽；(C) 運氣；(D) 壓力

2. 駕駛自用車是氣候變遷的促成因素之一，因為車輛會產生大量的溫室氣體。
   (A) 衣架；(B) 法庭；(C) **因素**；(D) 成套工具

3. 我們新就任的總統出身卑微。他的父母來自低社會經濟的背景。
   (A) 立即地；(B) 仁慈地；(C) **卑微地**；(D) 完全地

4. 在家辦公或許是個好主意。這樣浪費在通勤的時間和金錢就會更少。
   (A) 儲存；(B) **浪費**；(C) 釋放；(D) 攜帶

5. 我跟理髮師有預約。我需要修剪我的頭髮。
   (A) 律師；(B) 會計師；(C) **理髮師**；(D) 牙醫

6. Sharon 是一個非常直率的人，且從不猶豫告訴其他人她的想法。
   (A) 自私的；(B) **直率的**；(C) 優雅的；(D) 愛玩的

7. Rachel 和我度過了一個愉快的野餐時光。我們非常享受美食和風景。
   (A) 新鮮的；(B) 開放的；(C) 自然的；(D) **愉快的**

8. 政府應該採取有效的措施來提倡資源回收，以減少塑膠廢棄物。
   (A) 啞的；(B) 軍事的；(C) **有效的**；(D) 簡短的

9. 我前去找 Roberts 先生並問候他，但他卻忽略我並走開。
   (A) 變暗；(B) 剎車；(C) 關閉；(D) **忽略**

10. 昨晚，這個國家受到一個世紀以來最強的地震侵襲。
    (A) **襲擊**；(B) 防衛；(C) 批准；(D) 做記號

11. 去溯溪前要確實看過氣象預報。一場突如其來的陣雨會使河水迅速暴漲。
    (A) **天氣**；(B) 好運；(C) 選舉；(D) 液體

12. 臺北近郊的直升機墜毀意外導致好幾位高級軍官喪命，這是今日最為重大的一則新聞。
    (A) 影響；(B) **一則**；(C) 實例；(D) 器械

13. 街上的志工請人們慷慨捐款行公益，以支助窮困的人。
    (A) **慷慨地**；(B) 誠實地；(C) 流利地；(D) 失控地

14. 在西方社會，給服務生小費是一種習慣。
    (A) 對…課稅；(B) 放在…的上面；(C) **給小費**；(D) 繫

15. 當面對可能的危險時，蝸牛會退縮殼裡來保護自己。
    (A) 水流；(B) **殼**；(C) 蹤跡；(D) 蜂巢

II. Fill in the Blank

1. earth	2. weathered	3. butterflies
4. attach	5. being	

1. 你到底去哪了啊？我到處在找你。
   ★ 疑問詞 + on earth 到底，究竟

2. 經年累月，崎嶇不平的海岸受到海浪侵蝕，逐漸變成一片海蝕平臺。
   ★ weather 受到風雨侵蝕

3. 當我看到我喜歡的人朝我走過來時，我感到非常緊張。 ★ have butterflies (in sb's stomach)…感到非常緊張

4. 繳交申請表的時候需要附上一張你近期的照片。 ★ attach 附上

5. 雖然我不知道恐龍確切從何時開始存在，但我知道牠們大約在六千五百萬年前滅絕。
   ★ come into being 開始存在，誕生

III. Guided Translation

1. wound; around
2. rich; in
3. Draw; up
4. by; far
5. become; of

Review 2

I. Multiple Choice

1. D	2. D	3. C	4. A	5. B
6. C	7. C	8. B	9. B	10. D
11. C	12. C	13. B	14. A	15. D

1. 受損的腎臟對病患的健康造成危害，因此外科醫師將其移除，並替換一顆健康的。
   (A) 引用；(B) 治癒；(C) 忍受；**(D) 造成**

2. 你現在應該避免吃甜食，否則會破壞你吃晚餐的胃口。
   (A) 以…為目標；(B) 結合；(C) 狩獵；**(D) 避免**

3. 自從我和我哥哥起爭執後，我們之間就變得有些疏遠。我們不再跟對方講話了。
   (A) 進展；(B) 對話；**(C) 距離**；(D) 隧道

4. 其中一位不付錢的顧客給我們造成很多麻煩，所以我們決定採取法律行動。
   (A) 麻煩；(B) 榮譽；(C) 花費；(D) 創造

5. 這間教會創立於五十年前，自此它就一直是這個社區重要的一分子。
   (A) 找到；**(B) 創立**；(C) 資助；(D) 淹水

6. 觀測星象的時候，我總是嘗試記住它們彼此之間的位置關係。
   (A) 地區；(B) 結果；**(C) 關係**；(D) 回應

7. 你今晚不能和我們去看電影太可惜了。我覺得你會喜歡那部電影。
   (A) 愉悅；(B) 社會；**(C) 可惜**；(D) 趨勢

8. 當那群罪犯被關進牢裡時，正義獲得了伸張。
   (A) 建議；**(B) 正義**；(C) 信仰；(D) 誠實

9. 學生們得要個別操作實驗。團隊合作和與他人討論是不被允許的。
   (A) 真誠地；**(B) 個別地**；(C) 科學地；(D) 公開地

10. 根據我們的資料，我們有信心明年的利潤會變得更高。
    (A) 很棒的；(B) 基本的；(C) 相等的；**(D) 自信的**

11. 我不小心讓我的咖啡灑出來了，它在我的襯衫上留下一塊很大的黑漬。
    (A) 攪拌；(B) 微笑；**(C) 灑出**；(D) 嗅聞

12. 對 Joan 來說，當祕書是一件輕鬆的差事，而她打算找一份能有更多挑戰的工作。
    (A) 糨糊；(B) 薪水；**(C) 挑戰**；(D) 碳酸飲料

13. 我盡可能節儉地過生活，不讓我的生活開銷對父母造成煩擾。
    (A) 偽造；**(B) 煩擾**；(C) 僱用；(D) 依靠

14. 月臺上的乘客越來越不耐煩，因為火車已經誤點三十分鐘了。
    (A) 月臺；(B) 溝渠；(C) 範圍；(D) 包裹

15. Jenny 出門約會之前在鏡子前面端詳了自己。
    (A) 面具；(B) 餐巾；(C) 睡衣；**(D) 鏡子**

II. Fill in the Blank

1. call	2. nerves	3. feed
4. take	5. passed	

1. 時間很晚了，我也想睡了。我們今天就到此為止，現在就回家吧。
   ★ call it a day 到此為止；結束一天；收工

2. 如果 Lola 和 Nelson 在的話，我就不想待在這了。他們示愛的方式讓我覺得很煩。
   ★ get on sb's nerves 使某人心煩

3. 吸血蝙蝠以其他動物的血液為食。
   ★ feed on sth 以…為食

4. 我知道你現在很忙，但這份問卷只會花你一點時間。★ take up 占用 (時間)，費 (時)

5. Elizabeth 聽到她獨子的死訊時便昏倒了。
   ★ pass out 昏倒

III. Guided Translation

1. finding; fault
2. around; corner
3. in; motion
4. took; over
5. falling; apart

Review 3

I. Multiple Choice

1. B	2. A	3. D	4. B	5. B
6. B	7. B	8. A	9. D	10. A
11. C	12. C	13. B	14. C	15. A

1. 所有的員工都感到很挫折，因為他們已經三個月沒拿到薪水了，且他們無法聯繫上他們的僱主。
   (A) 喜悅的；(B) **挫折的**；(C) 休閒的；(D) 武裝的

2. 我換了座位以遠離那個呼吸帶有很重菸味的男生。
   (A) **呼吸**；(B) 事務；(C) 車棚；(D) 山頂

3. 記憶，就如同其他所有事物一般，會隨著歲月衰退。沒有東西本該永久留存。
   (A) 聚集；(B) 燃燒；(C) 摺疊；(D) **衰退**

4. 這個新興療法的研發具革命性。它將徹底地改變我們治療癌症的方式。
   (A) 令人反感的；(B) **革命性的**；(C) 離譜的；(D) 羨慕的

5. 政府官員宣布因為受到烏俄戰爭持續進行的影響，下週油價將會上漲。
   (A) 繫緊；(B) **宣布**；(C) 抱怨；(D) 要求

6. Preble 從五樓高的地方摔下來還完全沒有受傷，真是一個奇蹟。
   (A) 準則；(B) **奇蹟**；(C) 協定；(D) 懇求

7. 店員被訓練在收取鈔票之前做檢查以確認真偽。
   (A) 期待；(B) **檢查**；(C) 懷疑；(D) 探勘

8. 網路上關於性騷擾的故事喚起我自己在青少年時被騷擾的記憶。
   (A) **喚起**；(B) 埋葬；(C) 融入；(D) 發明

9. 有些動物會在夏天結束前收集食物，確保有足夠的存量過冬。
   (A) 明智的；(B) 固執的；(C) 真誠的；(D) **足夠的**

10. 我被過多的資訊給淹沒了，搞得我暈頭轉向。
    (A) **旋轉**；(B) 吐出；(C) 放置；(D) 滑動

11. Jason 能夠藉由觀察人們的身體語言來猜測他們當下的感受。
    (A) 等候；(B) 舉起；(C) **觀察**；(D) 打斷

12. 朱先生譴責他兒子魯莽的行為，並說此舉很容易導致衝突。
    (A) 虛構的故事；(B) 差事；(C) **行為**；(D) 加薪

13. 幫我轉到第十五臺。搖滾慈善音樂會正在現場轉播。
    (A) 爭論；(B) **轉播**；(C) 調整；(D) 禁止

14. Kelly 的醫生開了一些藥給她，並要她每六小時吃一顆。
    (A) 別針；(B) 深坑；(C) **藥丸**；(D) 堆

15. 所有學生恭敬地聆聽著這位剛獲得諾貝爾文學獎的客座講師。
    (A) **恭敬地**；(B) 得體地；(C) 分別地；(D) 相對地

II. Fill in the Blank

1. content	2. dispute	3. cunning
4. risk	5. tune	

1. 這位軍事強人不滿足於推翻執政的政府，還計畫要侵略鄰國。
   ★ be content with 對…感到滿意

2. 教育改革是否應在明年啟動仍在爭論中。
   ★ in dispute 在爭論中

3. 別相信 Saul 說的任何事情。他跟狐狸一樣狡猾。★ cunning 狡猾的

4. 空氣中的灰塵、花粉或動物毛髮會讓有過敏的人身處於風險之中。
   ★ at risk 處於危險，具風險

5. Woods 很不會唱歌。他總是會唱走音。
   ★ out of tune 走音

III. Guided Translation

1. under; arrest
2. at; mercy
3. class; reunion
4. impose; upon
5. profiting; from

Review 4

I. Multiple Choice

1. B	2. A	3. C	4. A	5. B
6. C	7. C	8. B	9. A	10. D
11. C	12. A	13. C	14. D	15. A

1. Jimmy 被指控從事不法行為。 為捍衛他的名譽，他以一篇嚴厲的聲明及法律訴訟來反駁他的指控者。
   (A) 使人想起；**(B) 反駁**；(C) 通知；(D) 增強

2. 所有的參賽者緊張地等待著最終結果。沒有人敢開口說話。
   (A) 最終的；(B) 過度的；(C) 永恆的；(D) 巨大的

3. 我們對新產品的潛在市場抱持樂觀態度。我們相信它會賣得很好，並產生可觀的利潤。
   (A) 合邏輯的；(B) 實際的；**(C) 潛在的**；(D) 中世紀的

4. Brolin 拒絕對關於近期的選舉做任何評論，因這是個高度敏感的主題。
   (A) 關於；(B) 減去；(C) 包括；(D) 與…對比

5. Bobby 聲稱他能夠透過看我的手相來幫我算命，但我認為這純粹是胡說八道。
   (A) 海軍；**(B) 手掌**；(C) 停止；(D) 大腿

6. 我哥哥在我打完棒球比賽回家後，切了一條麵包為我做一些三明治。
   (A) 一串 (葡萄等)；(B) 大量；**(C) 一條 (麵包)**；(D) 女用襯衫

7. 不要一下吃這麼多年糕。它們不易被消化。
   (A) 圖解；(B) 下沉；**(C) 消化**；(D) 增添風味

8. 我的老師對我的作文不滿意，並要求我修改。
   (A) 註冊；**(B) 修改**；(C) 撤退；(D) 復仇

9. 每個人都坐下後，主席接著宣布這場會議的目標。
   (A) 接著做；(B) 較喜歡；(C) 仔細看；(D) 擦亮

10. Rick 在食用一顆有毒的蘑菇後感到非常不適，必須馬上送往醫院。
    (A) 可攜的；(B) 熱情的；(C) 先前的；**(D) 有毒的**

11. 記得在火烤牛排之前撒上一些鹽和研磨胡椒。
    (A) 蹣跚；(B) 顫抖；**(C) 撒**；(D) 舀出

12. Cecelia 打給我時把她的聲音裝成別人來對我惡作劇，但我知道那是她。
    (A) 喬裝；(B) (強制) 執行；(C) 透露；(D) 害怕

13. 缺乏強烈的動機，要學生獨立自主地學習是不容易的。
    (A) 地標；(B) 運作；**(C) 動機**；(D) 中級學生

14. 有些心理學家相信多元智慧的概念，認為人們能以不同的方式展現智慧。
    (A) 中等的；(B) 誤導的；(C) 悲慘的；**(D) 多數的**

15. 我們新設計的帳篷有各種的形狀與尺寸供您挑選。
    (A) 各種的；(B) 單一的；(C) 快速的；(D) 需要照顧的

II. Fill in the Blank

1. drain	2. advantage	3. hasty
4. baggage	5. partial	

1. 這個國家突然遭受經濟蕭條，許多人的投資付之東流。★ down the drain 付諸東流

2. 敵軍的攻勢正在瓦解，現在進攻對我們來說是有利的。★ to sb's advantage 對…有利的

3. 別草率評斷一個人。 完全了解一個人需要時間。★ be hasty in 草率做…

4. 在通過機場海關前，記得要領取你的行李。
   ★ baggage 行李

5. Conan 抱怨父母對他妹妹偏心。他認為他們對她的愛勝於他。★ be partial to 偏好…

III. Guided Translation

1. on; alert
2. nursery; rhyme
3. relevant; to
4. rebel; against
5. fall; categories

Review 5

I. Multiple Choice

1. A	2. A	3. B	4. B	5. D
6. A	7. D	8. D	9. B	10. A
11. C	12. A	13. C	14. D	15. D

1. 我們需要在旺季的時候多僱幾位助理來幫忙店裡。
   (A) **助理**；(B) 導演；(C) 戰士；(D) 輸家

2. 在一週要結束的時候，當 George 想起過去這幾天所有發生在他身上的好事時，他感到一陣滿足。
   (A) **想起**；(B) 澄清；(C) 從⋯奪去；(D) 引發

3. 我的提案被回絕了，因為我沒能說服主管們認為它值得花時間與金錢。
   (A) 操控；(B) **說服**；(C) 擾亂；(D) 增加

4. 人們經常與才剛認識的人倉促進入關係，而忽略了潛在的危險訊號。
   (A) 克服；(B) **忽略**；(C) 超過；(D) 推翻

5. 越來越多人選擇住在城市，以享有都市生活的便利。
   (A) 底下的；(B) 普遍的；(C) 緊急的；(D) **都市的**

6. 由於內戰，許多難民逃離他們的國家，並在偏僻的難民營過著隔離與貧困的生活好幾年了。
   (A) **隔離**；(B) 演示；(C) 重要；(D) 結合

7. 在大學，你不需要教授的許可便可離開教室。
   (A) 神祕；(B) 機會；(C) 反應；(D) **許可**

8. 人類的正常體溫約為攝氏三十五到三十七度。
   (A) 主要的；(B) 次要的；(C) 種族的；(D) **正常的**

9. 我喜歡在閒暇時間讀小說、看 YouTube 影片、彈吉他或去散步。
   (A) 把手；(B) **閒暇**；(C) 本地人；(D) 工業

10. 獨角獸是只存在於傳說和奇幻故事中的虛構生物。
    (A) **虛構的**；(B) 極大的；(C) 富想像力的；(D) 即將到來的

11. 牛仔褲是由一種稱做丹寧布的耐用織品製成的，因此它們不容易磨損。
    (A) 最新的；(B) 不停的；(C) **耐用的**；(D) 舊時的

12. 經過樹叢的時候，我的雙手和臉都被鋒利的葉子刮傷了。
    (A) **刮傷**；(B) 蔑視；(C) 爭搶；(D) 散開

13. 廚房裡散發著淡淡的咖啡香，喚起我想喝杯咖啡的渴望。
    (A) 狹窄地；(B) 嚴重地；(C) **微弱地**；(D) 正式地

14. 南極洲是一塊位於地球最南端的大陸，上面大多處於冰封的狀態。
    (A) 國土的主體；(B) 沙漠；(C) 海洋；(D) **大陸**

15. Norton 每週將他剩下的零用錢存入銀行，逐年下來已經積蓄了一大筆存款。
    (A) 鑄幣廠；(B) 屬性；(C) 擋風玻璃；(D) **存款**

II. Fill in the Blank

1. crept	2. vacancies	3. laundry
4. blinking	5. species	

1. 小偷肯定是趁我睡覺時潛入家裡的，因為我根本不知道我家被闖入了。★ creep into 潛入

2. 下週將舉行一場選舉，以填補委員會裡的兩個空缺。★ vacancy (職位) 空缺

3. 在洗衣機被發明之前，人們得親手洗衣服。★ do the laundry 洗衣服

4. 當印表機的燈號停止閃爍時，就代表它準備好執行下一個任務了。★ blink 閃爍

5. 環境運動分子呼籲政府採取行動保護瀕危物種。★ species (生物分類) 種

III. Guided Translation

1. romantic; atmosphere
2. fossil; fuels
3. memorial; hall
4. distribution; goods
5. conservative; attitude

Review 6

I. Multiple Choice

1. B	2. C	3. D	4. D	5. A
6. A	7. D	8. D	9. A	10. D
11. C	12. B	13. C	14. D	15. B

1. 經過六週的育兒假後，Sam 如今已準備重返教職。
   (A) 假定；**(B) 重返**；(C) 以為；(D) 攝取

2. Wazowski 總統從沒有料想到他所僱用的私人軍事公司的首領會成為他的反對者並威脅到他的政權。
   (A) 贊助者；(B) 難民；**(C) 反對者**；(D) 傳教士

3. 即便 Dike 的部隊很明顯地毫無勝算可言，他仍堅持要他的手下進攻。
   (A) 協助；(B) 反抗；(C) 存在於；**(D) 堅持**

4. Cindy 在準備捉弄老師的時候，臉上露出了搗蛋的笑容。
   (A) 進步的；(B) 樂觀的；(C) 貧窮的；**(D) 搗蛋的**

5. 當 Blake 和 Will 試著爬過圍欄的時候，他們的褲子被尖銳的金屬線劃破。
   (A) 劃破；(B) 拉上拉鍊；(C) 啜飲；(D) 滴下

6. 派對過後，我家整個一團糟。被丟棄的瓶子散落各處。
   (A) 丟棄；(B) 用帶子繫；(C) 駁斥；(D) 祝福

7. 不要把鐘當作禮物送給華人。它在中華文化象徵死亡。
   (A) 維持；(B) 冒犯；(C) 提及；**(D) 象徵**

8. Robin 剛到這個國家，對其習俗不太熟悉，但藉由觀察在地人的作為並跟著效仿，他適應得不錯。
   (A) 也就是說；(B) 否則；(C) 同時；**(D) 同樣地**

9. Holmes 錯誤地認定女性無法理性思考，這讓他的觀點帶有嚴重的偏見。
   (A) 使有偏見；(B) 給予特權；(C) 開藥；(D) 察覺

10. Norman 無法抗拒鄉村生活的誘人魅力，決定搬到臺東。
    (A) 地震；(B) 抽筋；(C) 暴動；**(D) 誘惑**

11. 下跌的年度收益導致公共支出縮減。
    (A) 供品；(B) 前任；**(C) 收益**；(D) 裁判

12. 攀登聖母峰是為十足的挑戰，但遠征隊堅持不懈，最終登頂。
    (A) 動員；**(B) 堅持**；(C) 抗議；(D) 統治

13. 經過多年的反目成仇，兩位鄰居終於和解。
    (A) 過度；(B) 激發；**(C) 使和解**；(D) 居住於

14. 此案被稱作世紀案件，因為其結果將為未來類似的案件開設先例。
    (A) 總統任期；(B) 預測；(C) 螺旋槳；**(D) 先例**

15. Logan 將嗅鹽靠近 Megan 的鼻孔以讓她恢復意識。
    (A) 肺；**(B) 鼻孔**；(C) 肋骨；(D) 青春痘

II. Fill in the Blank

1. compensation	2. relays	3. racked
4. thrives	5. stake	

1. Billy 的車被馬路上突然出現的天坑吞沒而報銷了。他獲得了新臺幣十萬元的賠償。
   ★ in compensation for 作為⋯的賠償

2. 員工得輪班工作以確保機器整晚運轉順暢。
   ★ in relays 輪班；接力

3. 我已經絞盡腦汁了，可是我還是沒辦法想出任何好點子。★ rack sb's brain(s) 絞盡腦汁

4. Jane 善於面對壓力，但與她不同的是，我壓力太大的時候無法工作。★ thrive on 善於⋯

5. 在暴風雨中派遣救難直升機的決定將機組員的性命暴露於風險之中。
   ★ at stake 處於危險中

III. Guided Translation

1. in; miniature
2. keep; perspective
3. filling; prescription
4. on; threshold
5. vitamin; supplements

Review 7

I. Multiple Choice

1. A	2. D	3. B	4. D	5. A
6. A	7. B	8. B	9. C	10. D
11. A	12. A	13. A	14. C	15. A

1. 在表演的過程中，強烈的音樂從揚聲器擴大出來，觀眾的情緒都非常澎湃。
   (A) **擴大**；(B) 減少；(C) 偽造；(D) 保護

2. 經過多年的時間，Dean 已與他的每一個生意夥伴培養出穩固的關係。
   (A) 單調的；(B) 地理的；(C) 東方的；(D) **堅固的**

3. 這種壓力疾病造成的持續性頭痛可長達數週之久。
   (A) 全面的；(B) **持續的**；(C) 非常危險的；(D) 不免一死的

4. 一連串的貪汙醜聞促使數名高級政府官員辭職下臺。
   (A) 溝槽；(B) 雕像；(C) 馬鞍；(D) **醜聞**

5. Carl 和 Carmen 在療養勝地度過他們的假期，享受水療、按摩和養生食物。
   (A) **度假勝地**；(B) 山崩；(C) 碼頭；(D) 果園

6. 我的決定絕非魯莽。我實際上是經過仔細思索後才下定決心的。
   (A) **魯莽的**；(B) 不誠實的；(C) 古怪的；(D) 不易改變的

7. 得知這麼多難民在試圖橫渡地中海時溺斃讓 Brian 感到悲痛。
   (A) 裝飾；(B) **悲痛**；(C) 傷害；(D) 使聽不見

8. 小憩三十分鐘後，我恢復了活力，並準備好迎接下午的課程。
   (A) 感到遺憾；(B) **恢復活力**；(C) 代替；(D) 限制

9. 如果工作讓你感到疲累，為何不去休假個一星期呢？
   (A) 暫緩；(B) 宣判…有罪；(C) **使疲憊**；(D) 使驚慌害怕

10. Smith 在連續開了六小時的車之後視線開始變得模糊，所以他前往服務區休息一下。
    (A) 搖擺；(B) 打噴嚏；(C) 壓迫；(D) **模糊**

11. 這一只老舊的機械錶對我而言具有情感價值。它是我已故的外婆送給我的禮物。
    (A) **情感的**；(B) 資深的；(C) 凶殘的；(D) 膚淺的

12. Janet 極度迷信，她相信在晚上吹口哨和用手指月亮會招致厄運。
    (A) **迷信的**；(B) 謹慎的；(C) 熱中的；(D) 主導的

13. 我們的調查顯示四位孩童當中就有一位在學校受到霸凌，突顯了教導孩子尊重和自我保護的重要性。
    (A) **欺負**；(B) 排放；(C) 調整；(D) 繁殖

14. 新建的禮堂能容納五千人，並能用來舉行各種藝文活動。
    (A) 水族館；(B) 大道；(C) **禮堂**；(D) 金字塔

15. 要求學生把上衣紮進褲子或裙子裡的校規早已過時且應被廢除。
    (A) **把…塞入**；(B) 捲動 (頁面)；(C) 倒入 (液體)；(D) 投擲

II. Fill in the Blank

1. spur	2. brace	3. saddled
4. Discriminating	5. rash	

1. Josh 做事總是一時興起，而沒有事先規劃。
   ★ on the spur of the moment 一時興起

2. 我們國家需為缺水做好準備，因為我們進入了旱季。★ brace oneself for 做好…準備

3. 我們對那個新進員工感到同情，因為她要負責面對挑剔的顧客。
   ★ saddle sb with sth 使某人承擔某事

4. 歧視人們的種族與性傾向是可恥且不法的。
   ★ discriminate against 歧視

5. 過去幾週我們不斷地接到關於交通惡化的抱怨。★ a rash of (壞事等) 接連發生

III. Guided Translation

1. conceive; of
2. substitute; for
3. derived; from
4. emotional; trauma
5. vicious; circle/cycle

Review 8

I. Multiple Choice

1. D	2. B	3. B	4. C	5. A
6. D	7. C	8. C	9. A	10. D
11. C	12. C	13. B	14. A	15. B

1. 對 Tina 來說，受邀到以前就讀的大學系所演講著實為一個讚美。
   (A) 魅力；(B) 評估；(C) 估算；**(D) 讚美**

2. 一群毒梟在正要準備進行一場非法買賣的時候被警方逮捕。
   (A) 拿取；**(B) 實行**；(C) 仔細思考；(D) 交換

3. Keisha 的教授請她以實例來闡明她對這個概念的理解。
   (A) 解放；**(B) 詳述**；(C) 使交替；(D) 抬高

4. 飢餓的狼群追捕到了一頭鹿，並在數分鐘之內將之吞噬殆盡。
   (A) 腐敗；(B) 使痛苦；**(C) 吞噬光**；(D) 使厭惡

5. 謠傳這間廢棄的豪宅內有屋主的鬼魂出沒。
   (A) (幽靈) 出沒於；(B) 哀悼；(C) 隱瞞；(D) 背叛

6. 許多法學院的學生對於近期一系列法庭片當中律師被刻板印象化的呈現方式感到不悅。
   (A) 擦傷；(B) 奪取；(C) 庇護；**(D) 刻板地看待**

7. 種族歧視者是一種會對與之不同的種族懷有敵意態度的人。
   (A) 陶器的；(B) 善交際的；**(C) 有敵意的**；(D) 高尚的

8. 好幾名國會成員因收賄被逮，引起了一連串的輿論撻伐。
   (A) 鱒魚；(B) (精神) 折磨；**(C) 連發**；(D) 象徵

9. 經過兩年的戰事，大家都對於這場無意義的戰爭感到厭倦，但似乎卻沒有結束的辦法。
   (A) 疲倦的；(B) 怪異的；(C) 邪惡的；(D) 小心的

10. Pierce 對於究竟要跟爸媽住還是租一間公寓以享有個人隱私感到兩難。
    (A) 尺寸；(B) 診斷；(C) 令人分心的事；**(D) 進退兩難**

11. 數百名警力包圍了立法院，不讓抗議者進出。
    (A) 安定；(B) 壯麗；**(C) 包圍**；(D) 繼承

12. 有些地球上最奇特的物種獨有於澳洲。其他地方皆找不到。
    (A) 傲慢地；(B) 象徵地；**(C) 獨有地**；(D) 憤慨地

13. 奇蹟似地，這尊女神的雕像未受損傷，而廟裡的其他東西皆在火災中付之一炬。
    (A) 堅持的；**(B) 未受損傷的**；(C) 同樣的；(D) 創新的

14. 這兩個國家終於在多年的對立之後恢復外交的關係。
    (A) 外交的；(B) 同等的；(C) 嘲諷的；(D) 輕微的

15. 我們沒預期到溫度會驟降，所以沒有帶足夠的保暖衣物。
    (A) 外向的；**(B) 突然的**；(C) 無限的；(D) 豐富的

II. Fill in the Blank

1. granted	2. excluded	3. diameter
4. suspension	5. dwelling	

1. Russell 跪下並自願進行這場探險，而國王同意了他的請求。★ grant 同意

2. 學生不應被排除在校務討論之外，因為他們是一所學校的主體。★ exclude from 排除

3. 你可以幫我把那個圓變大嗎？我需要直徑十英尺的大小。★ in diameter 直徑 (多少單位)

4. Helen 很怕走吊橋，因為她害怕自己可能會跌落。★ suspension bridge 吊橋

5. 別再老扒著過去的錯誤不放。木已成舟。該是向前看的時候了。★ dwell on sth 老是想著某事

III. Guided Translation

1. apt; to
2. Verbal; abuse
3. compatible; with
4. nonprofit; organization
5. on; impulse

PLUS 1

I. Multiple Choice

1. C	2. A	3. B	4. A	5. D
6. B	7. C	8. B	9. C	10. C
11. A	12. A	13. C	14. D	15. D

1. David 過度保護的父母讓他感到窒息，他希望自己上大學的時候能夠離開家。
(A) 使鎮靜；(B) 裁判；**(C) 使窒息**；(D) 旋轉

2. 政府官員不能在沒有國會批准的情況下推行任何法律。
(A) 批准；(B) 分期付款；(C) 救贖；(D) 獨創力

3. 有了網路，我們不需要使用天線便可觀賞數百個頻道。
(A) 下水道；**(B) 天線**；(C) 流浪漢；(D) 沙沙聲

4. 強風與暴雨使得屋舍和電線桿傾倒，在僅僅數小時內便造成數千萬的損失。
(A) 傾倒；(B) 隆隆作響；(C) 傳播 (思想)；(D) 用扣環扣住

5. 下坡行駛於彎曲路段時記得要放慢車速，否則你很容易跌落道路兩側。
(A) 殘忍的；(B) 被壓抑的；(C) 單調乏味的；**(D) 彎曲的**

6. 身為一位有企圖心的女性，Margret 不喜歡放棄職涯去當家庭主婦的前景。
(A) 覬覦；**(B) 喜歡**；(C) 撥彈 (琴弦)；(D) 嘲笑

7. 在我們到訪峇里島的時候，我們幾乎每天早上都在市集裡溜達，探索具有異國情調的商品。
(A) 暴風雪；(B) 辮子；**(C) 市集**；(D) 氣壓計

8. 在一場小雨之後，空氣變得清新了，而隨著天空放晴，萬物閃閃發光。
(A) 胸針；**(B) 毛毛雨**；(C) (籬笆) 圈地；(D) 髮型

9. Zelda 的父親勸阻她不要出國讀書，說他負擔不起。
(A) 曲解事實；(B) 不信任；**(C) 勸阻**；(D) 派遣

10. 人們以譏笑的方式蔑視 Samuel，因他們不覺得他取得事業成功的手段是正當的。
(A) 一劑藥量；(B) 協定；**(C) 譏笑**；(D) 輕微震動

11. 街道上和公園裡的流浪狗可以是一種公共威脅。牠們可能會攻擊人，尤其是孩童。
(A) 威脅；(B) 困境；(C) 尖頂；(D) 軼事

12. 去海灘消遣的人四肢攤開躺在海灘椅上，讓他們的皮膚做日光浴。
(A) 四肢攤平；(B) 惡化；(C) 釀造；(D) 摸索

13. Lawrence 的親友在聽到他獲得去加州大學洛杉磯分校訪問的獎學金時都欣喜若狂。
(A) 盔甲；(B) 閒聊；**(C) 欣喜若狂**；(D) 用小火煮

14. 住在鄉村地區的其中一項缺點就是公共運輸的品質甚差。
(A) 儀式；(B) 成分；(C) 預兆；**(D) 缺點**

15. 食品製造商應該遵守食品安全規範，這有助於保護消費者的健康。
(A) 戳洞；(B) 撫摸；(C) 無視；**(D) 保護**

II. Fill in the Blank

1. streak	2. propped	3. fiddling
4. stunt	5. flutter	

1. Samson 的個性有點心不在焉。 儘管你跟他說話時他會回覆，但你可以感覺到他的魂飄走了。★ a streak of 性格有些…(的傾向)

2. Rina 把吉他撐在大腿上，彈奏一些民謠歌曲來娛樂她的賓客。
★ prop sth on sth 將某物支撐於某物上

3. 當 Ethan 的主管在質問他的工作表現時，他不斷翻弄他的領帶。★ fiddling with sth 撥弄某物

4. 一位知名演員被目擊在無任何保護措施的情況下攀爬一棟建築物，而人們懷疑他耍這個噱頭的動機為何。★ pull a stunt 做愚蠢冒險的事

5. Gordon 自從他的妻子突然生病並被送至外科病房後就處在慌亂之中。
★ in a flutter 慌亂，緊張

III. Guided Translation

1. made; blunder
2. eroded; away
3. came; in/into; vogue
4. displeased; with
5. globbled; up

PLUS 2

I. Multiple Choice

1. B	2. B	3. C	4. A	5. D
6. D	7. A	8. C	9. A	10. A
11. A	12. B	13. D	14. C	15. B

1. 在某些國家，人們被允許使用包含致命武力在內的一切必要手段來對付任何入侵其私有土地的人。
   (A) 著手從事；**(B) 入侵 (私有地)**；(C) 使陷入困境；(D) 俯身

2. 我的祖母在經過腸胃手術之後看起來疲累且虛弱。
   (A) 和藹可親的；**(B) 虛弱的**；(C) 虔誠的；(D) (語氣) 強調的

3. 你再這樣對別人嘮叨下去會惹人厭的。
   (A) 動脈；(B) 槳；**(C) 令人討厭的人**；(D) 代言人

4. Aaron 在電視節目上涉及他人性傾向的低俗笑話受到大眾的嚴厲批評。
   (A) 低俗的；(B) 獲勝的；(C) 黯淡的；(D) 見多識廣的

5. Nixon 要他的手下各就各位，然後等待著敵對幫派走入他們的圈套。
   (A) 飢荒；(B) 酒館；(C) 火光閃耀；**(D) 圈套**

6. 在《寂靜的春天》中，作者 Rachel Carson 告誡讀者關於過度使用殺蟲劑對環境所帶來的負面影響。
   (A) 暴風雨；(B) 盜獵者；(C) 宗族；**(D) 殺蟲劑**

7. 希臘人包圍了特洛伊城好幾年都無法占領該地，直到他們以特洛伊木馬設局欺騙了特洛伊人。
   (A) 包圍；(B) 輕彈；(C) 激怒；(D) 啄食

8. 一個陌生人示意 Ginny 跟著他走。她表示拒絕並馬上離開。
   (A) 授予；(B) 表達惋惜；**(C) 示意**；(D) 使困惑

9. 當我父親在觀賞他最喜歡的喜劇時，我可以聽到他在咯咯笑。
   (A) 咯咯地笑；(B) 移居；(C) 為⋯寫序；(D) 在心中描繪

10. 如果你刪掉這些多餘的表達，你這篇文章就會變得好讀許多。
    (A) 冗餘的；(B) 好戰的；(C) 備用的；(D) 節儉的

11. 這兩國之間的關係曾是很親善的，但現在他們變成了敵人。
    (A) 熱誠的；(B) 附帶的；(C) (食物) 酥脆的；(D) 勇敢的

12. 普遍而言，宗教信仰教導人們去原諒而非報復。
    (A) 攪拌；**(B) 報復**；(C) 刪減；(D) 終結

13. 當 Britney 聽到這首舞曲時，她忍不住跟著節奏律動搖擺。
    (A) 粗壯的；(B) 醇熟的；(C) 歇斯底里的；**(D) 有節奏的**

14. 教師的匱乏在這個國家的某些偏遠地區是一個持續存在的問題，因為大部分的老師不願到那邊教書。
    (A) 制定法律；(B) 物質主義；**(C) 不足**；(D) 教養

15. Nicholas 所有的家庭成員都在納粹政權實施的大屠殺中喪命了。
    (A) 代替；**(B) 大屠殺**；(C) 紀念；(D) 重複出現

II. Fill in the Blank

1. temperament	2. tariffs	3. stammer
4. glistened	5. shuddered	

1. Elijah 的性情非常輕鬆。在他身旁總是會感到很自在。★ temperament 性情

2. 若我們不是這個自由貿易實體的會員，我們的出口商品在進入其會員國時就會面臨關稅。★ tariff 關稅

3. 小時候有結巴的人往往會受到同儕嘲弄，因而可能變得較沒有自信。★ stammer 結巴

4. Kilmer 在陽光底下打排球的時候，他的身體因著汗水閃閃發光。★ glisten with 因⋯閃閃發光

5. 一想到如果沒有準時繳交作業的話會有什麼後果，就讓我不寒而慄。★ shudder 發抖

III. Guided Translation

1. clutched; at
2. political; asylum
3. throbs; with
4. gulp; down
5. held; ransom

跨閱英文

王信雲 編著　　車畇庭 審定

學習不限於書本上的知識，而是「**跨**」出去，學習帶得走的能力！

跨文化
呈現不同的國家或文化，進而了解及尊重多元文化。

跨世代
橫跨時間軸，經歷不同的世代，見證其發展里程碑。

跨領域
整合兩個或兩個以上領域之間的知識，拓展知識領域。

1. 以新課綱的核心素養為主軸
網羅 3 大面向——「跨文化」、「跨世代」、「跨領域」，共 24 篇文章，引發你對各項議題的好奇。包含多元文化、家庭、生涯規劃、科技、資訊、性別平等、生命、閱讀素養、戶外、環境、海洋、防災等之多項重要議題，開拓多元領域的視野！

2. 跨出一板一眼的作答舒適圈
以循序漸進的實戰演練，搭配全彩的圖像設計，引導學生跳脫形式學習，練出「混合題型」新手感，並更進一步利用「進階練習」的訓練，達到整合知識和活用英文的能力。最後搭配「延伸活動」，讓你在各式各樣的活動中 *FUN* 學英文！

3. 隨書附贈活動式設計解析本
自學教學兩相宜，方便你完整對照中譯，有效理解文章，並有詳細的試題解析，讓你擊破各個答題關卡，從容應試每一關！

實戰新多益：全真模擬題本 3 回

SIWONSCHOOL LANGUAGE LAB ／著
戴瑜亭／譯

ETS 認證多益英語測驗專業發展工作坊講師
李海碩、張秀帆 真心推薦

本書特色

特色 1：單回成冊
揮別市面多數多益題本的厚重感，單回裝訂仿照真實測驗，提前適應答題手感。

特色 2：錯題解析
解析本提供深度講解，針對正確答案與誘答選項進行解題，全面掌握答題關鍵。

特色 3：誤答筆記
提供筆記模板，協助深入了解誤答原因，歸納出專屬於自己的學習筆記。

★試題音檔最多元★
實體光碟、線上音檔、多國口音、整回音檔、單題音檔

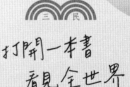